MW01614932

How Would Jesus Vote?

Published by How U Thinking Publishing Co.

Copyright 2008 by Kevin Armstrong

Scripture quotation are from the
The King James Version of the bible
Word definitions are taken from Webster's Dictionary

For More Information:
HOW U THINKING PU-
BISHING CO.
2157 MCCULLOUGH
BLVD. SUITE C TUPELO,
MS 38801

How Would Jesus Vote?

Introduction
Believers in Christ Preparing for the Polls

The title of the book is "How would Jesus Vote?", not "Who would Jesus Vote?". Far too often believers have gotten caught up in the carnality of the political process that tends to support the "status quo" and not follow the principles outlined in God's word concerning making decisions.

Whenever we go to the polls and cast votes for the next candidates that are positioning themselves to assume the tremendous responsibility of leadership, it seems not to give much promise in creating any different results than what we've had in previous years. If the hearts of the new leadership cannot be turned by the Lord, the results will be the same or maybe worse. This book is written primarily to those who believe that Jesus Christ is the Son of God and that His person still has a place in politics and our society. Many of the principles that this nation was founded upon, those that made this nation great, were placed in the hearts of many of the founding fathers by the Lord Himself.

This book titled *"How would Jesus Vote?"* was given to me by the Lord prior to the 2004 election with the intention that I would blow the proverbial trumpet in Zion concerning our (that is, believers in Jesus) responsibility to do our part to ensure that the person best suited for the position not based on race, gender or party affiliation would be given the opportunity to fulfill their role and duties according to the Lord's order of governing. Notice that I said the person best suited for the job.

Who only knows that person? The same per-

3

son who at the foundation of this great nation placed in many of the hearts of the framers of the constitution the desire to raise up a nation that would signify true liberty and give God the glory. This same person, although He may have lost some of His place as Lord in America, is still Lord of all the earth.

Much of what has been lost is because of the lethargy and the utter laziness that exists among believers in Jesus, we stood by and let the enemies of that which is right and holy take the benefit of righteousness and holiness from us. Many of those things we will discuss in this writing.

The purpose of the book is not to sway you one way or another in any election, but to convince and convict you as a believer in Jesus that you have the responsibility to vote not just for a particular political party or a particular race or gender but vote following your conscience. That which is right and holy based upon the word of God. I hope that the reader will find his or her way from the left or the right to the center in the political process because Christ is that center. It is designed to serve as a voting guide for the believers in Jesus not just in America but everywhere throughout the world where citizens have a right and privilege to exercise their voice in who is elected to govern their affairs.

HOW WOULD JESUS VOTE?

TABLE OF CONTENTS

INTRODUCTION

CHAPTER 1
Political VS. Moral

Politics is defined as theory and practice of government. The word *theory is* defined as *speculation: abstract thought* or *contemplation, an idea formed by speculation: an idea of* or *belief about something arrived at through speculation* or *conjecture.* This definition alone should cause concern for the believer.

Politics rules the world. America is a part of the world; a very big part, I might add. The condition of much of the world can almost always be traced to its political (governmental) structure. Let's take, for example, the tyrant dictator Sadaam Hussein. He used his political power to benefit himself and those he chose too. His two sons and a host of other relatives and friends were the benefactors of his position. Everyone else had to walk a very thin line making sure not to get off of that line, because if someone did he could be either murdered or imprisoned. This style of politics created a very dark period and loss of morality within the leadership and the consequential loss of hope within the citizenry. The long-lasting civil war in the African Nation of Sudan where hundreds of thousands of innocent people have been murdered or made refuges all because of some person's desire *to practice a theory developed through speculation and or conjecture.*

This great nation of ours falls in the same categories mentioned here. The structure of our government was established at the inception of this nation, founded upon many of the principles that were taken out of the Bible. Adherence to those principles is the reason that America became the greatest nation in the world, also known as a Christian nation. Where have we gone? What are we doing now? There are other nations who have fallen to a similar state and must answer these questions as well. If a nation is governed by those who gain their beliefs through speculation and or conjecture and then spend taxpayer monies to legislate and *practice* their theory, it is no wonder why our Christian America has fallen to such a state.

Believing is an act of the will: (What politicians believe)

We usually act in accordance with what we believe. Regardless of what politicians say, they will most certainly do what they believe. Jesus declared that there were those who spoke one way about Him, but their heart was far from him. In most campaigns in every level of government there are many promises made by candidates seeking election. When they are elected, they usually abandon the very foundation of what their campaign was about. This is due to the reality that we usually act in accordance to what we believe. There are many words that define belief: none of which conveys God's mindset of belief like this one in particular which Strong's Concordance states that *belief* is defined as "What I think to be true". Notice it's what I think to be true, not what someone else thinks to be true.

If any government is dominated by those who through theory practice government (politics), then most leaders are leading based on *their* beliefs, not the truth of God's word. The church is supposed to be composed of Christian believers, but many of them have fallen prey to what these politicians say they BELIEVE, and unfortunately, we find out when it's too late that what they put into practice is what they really believe. And it's usually far from what they said they believed. Which validates the point earlier made that we will always act in a manner based upon what we believe. This book is written with a hope that the Christian church all over the world will take its place in society, not the passive non-caring role that it has assumed for quite some time now. It is the believer in Jesus' responsibility to do their own due diligence to seek God's face and then cast a vote that will put the right person in the position to legislate according to God's order.

I am convinced that many believers are very ignorant about the political process. I don't use the word ignorant in a derogatory manner but rather a way to describe the detriment that has come to the believer because of our lack of knowledge concerning the political process. Many of us have been either too spiritual with the mindset that God isn't into politics, or too carnal to try to gain an understanding of God's place in politics. Others have taken the position of "why vote, my one vote won't matter". They're going to do what they want to anyway," etc.… Neither of these positions describes the mindset of an informed, responsible believer who refuses to be deceived by the enemy not man, as he masquerades his agenda through wicked politicians seeking self-gain.

Due to the believer's lack of involvement in the political process there are many areas of government that it will be difficult to find any real Christian influence. Influence is the light and salt of the world that Jesus said the believer is. This lack of Christian influence in government has made it possible for many of the other spheres of influence to have this lack of presence in them as well. Just to name a couple, the first is the business world. This sphere is dominated by those who don't claim Jesus as Lord and Savior and they use much of their resources on a lifestyle that doesn't glorify God. When there is no presence of light there is only darkness, the darkness will never be affected. In John 1, he writes that the light shined in the darkness and the darkness comprehended it not. Light always has a positive effect on darkness. Wherever light is darkness is not. This is why Jesus declared that the believer is the light of the world.

The second area is the entertainment world. Thank God for people like Matt Crouch at Trinity Broadcasting Network, The Kendrick Brothers and others who have endeavored to enter this dark world and offer some light where all sorts of evil are being propagated and the masses pay their hard-earned monies to sit in a theater, rent the DVD or a video on demand (VOD).

If a nation considers itself a Christian nation it would be obvious to me that there should be Christian leaders involved in and making a positive difference in every area of influence. It would appear that this could be the reason why we have lost and are losing so many of the liberties that the Lord has intended for us to enjoy.

The book of Romans 8:30-39 and Jeremiah 29: 11-14 paint a picture of a victorious and glorious church not defeated and victimized, but one who has a victorious outcome.

The apostle and the prophet's declarations are:
30 moreover whom he did predestinate, them he also called: and whom he called, them he also justified: and whom he justified, them he also glorified.: 31 What shall we then say to these things? If God be for us, who can be against us? 32

He that spared not his own Son, but delivered him up for us all, how shall he not with him also freely give us all things? 33 Who shall lay anything to the charge of God's elect? It is God that justifies. 34 Who is he that condemneth? It is Christ that died, yea rather, that is risen again, who is even at the right the hand of the God, who also maketh intercession for us. 35 Who shall separate us from the love of Christ? shall tribulation, or distress, or persecution, or famine, or nakedness, or peril, or sword? 36 As it is written, for thy sake we are killed all the day long; we are accounted as sheep for the slaughter. 37 Nay, in all these things we are more than conquerors through him that loved us. 38 For I am persuaded, that neither death, nor life, nor angels, nor principalities, nor powers, nor things present, nor things to come, 39 Nor height, nor depth, nor any other creature, shall be able to separate us from the love of God, which is in Christ Jesus our Lord.

Jeremiah 29:11-14 says:

"For I know the thoughts that I think toward you, saith the LORD, thoughts of peace, and not of evil, to give you an expected end. 12 Then shall ye call upon me, and ye shall go and pray unto me, and I will hearken unto you. 13 And ye shall seek me, and find me, when ye shall search for me with all/ your heart. 14 And I will be found of you, saith the LORD: and I will turn away your captivity, and I will gather you from all the nations, and from all the places whither I have driven you, saith the LORD; and I will bring you again into the place whence I caused you to be carried away captive.

These few verses of scripture give us a crystal-clear picture into the mindset of our Father God for His children. Let's take a look at Romans 8:37. Regardless of all of the negative things that were happening and had happened, the apostle says that we are still more than conquerors through Him (Christ) who love us. We must understand that our heavenly Father really does love us. As believers, we are never at the mercy of anyone except God Himself. His will is to always prosper us and give us a good future. But He requires that we involve ourselves in ***The Process.***

Through the act of compromising, the church has allowed God's established moral standard to be legislated right out from under our noses. I've heard some preachers say that you can't legislate morality but won't acknowledge that **THEY are** legislating immorality all over the nation in every level of government. Speaking of morality, morality is defined as: *That which is holy and right established by the word of God as accepted moral standard: standards of conduct that are accepted as right or proper*. This definition describes God's idea of righteousness and what many of the founding fathers had in mind when they set out to establish a government that would mirror God's order in government. A government that would be established in righteousness with acceptable moral standards that exemplify conduct that is accepted as right and/or proper as found in the greatest manuscript ever written: **THE BIBLE**.

Some may argue to the contrary concerning the rightness of many of the founding father's efforts in government because of the now-infamous slave trade by those who called themselves *Christians*, who stole a people from their country, their kindred, their father's house and ultimately their culture. Many generations of these African slaves were destroyed in the hulls of those ships during the travel from Africa to America and other parts of the world. It is crystal clear that those leaders who engaged in the slave trade made a grave error in judgment concerning these African men and women.

These catastrophic events did take place, but it doesn't nullify, and I will repeat myself that it doesn't nullify the intended plan and purpose of God to establish a government where one could worship God and be free to be all that God created him or her to be. What slavery did speak loud and clear as to how a man can get caught up in his own agenda after having heard from God as what to do or say reminiscent of our parents Adam and Eve. Adam and Eve's deception and failure did not cause God to change His mind about His original intent for mankind and He immediately puts into motion a plan to redeem mankind which was later fulfilled by the Seed of the Woman when He bruised the head of the serpent.

This ideal government (freedom to worship and exercise our inalienable rights in the earth) established many years ago came directly out of the mind of the creator himself. Within this clearly defined idea, there would be no need for speculation or conjecture concerning proper government. No need to practice, but rather put into place that which had already been established as the proper order. This system of government was and still is very clear and concise. If adhered to, there would be no doubt that it would produce the results intended by our Father God for His children. The current status of America as the wealthiest, the most powerful and the most Christian nation bears witness to the reality that there is a right way and a wrong way to do government even in the midst of those who do wrong.

Those who are in opposition to God's idea of government are attempting to redefine the constitution to validate their position so they can propagate their beliefs and do what they can to change it or give it a new language that fits their own agenda. At which time they'll find a political figurehead, someone who has the same beliefs. This person will gather as many campaign dollars as they can, alleging to legislate things that will benefit the constituents of his or her entire political party, but usually hiding his or her real agenda. A perfect example of this in America is the battle over the institution of marriage. There are states that have been pressed to change this institution to what they want it to be and many more are being pressed to change the oldest institution ever created: marriage between one man and one woman.

Who would have ever thought that the former governor of California, The Terminator, Arnold Schwarzenegger, would accept legislation against the institution of marriage, agreeing with those who say that the Bible is a discriminatory book and is not true. Because of this, homosexuals have the constitutional right to marry their partner of the same sex. What a travesty and a tragedy all wrapped up into one.

Every election will play a very vital role in how that county, city, state or nation progresses. The Bible is very clear on the subject concerning marriage. What should our position be? While those who hate God and His order are busy trying to rewrite the order, the church should be reminding them of what has been written, established and cannot and I do mean cannot be rewritten. God's word is not just written on paper, but it is written in the hearts and minds of His followers. We must take a different stand than we have in the past. We (Christians) must get involved in the political process and be even more adamant about what we BELIEVE, because we know that what we believe is right. After all we are the light of the world and the salt of the earth.

One of my heroes is Dr. Martin Luther King Jr. He epitomized what a person would do when he had a _conviction_ about what he believed. I thank God that He believed what the Bible had to say about morality. He was a man who left no question in the minds of many who heard him that the Word was written in his heart. Man was created in the image and likeness of God. Not just the white man or the black man, but all men, regardless of their skin color, are created equal, because God cannot and does not have respect of persons. No one race was created superior and another one inferior. Many have used the Bible to justify their prejudice but the order of God is sure and cannot be changed. Dr. King acknowledges the Bible as the final authority. Regardless of what it looked like, he still had a dream. If those who call themselves Christians would read the bible until it is written in their hearts and minds, the same fervor that Dr. King displayed will certainly produce the same results. Just the thought of a mass of believers living by their convictions fills my heart with joy.

Speaking of Dr. King, his 1954 sermon entitled "Rediscovering Lost Values", he speaks extensively on the subject of morality. This sermon more than validates my point concerning morality. I would encourage you to listen to the sermon in its entirety. Here's an excerpt

"I want you to think with me this morning from the subject: rediscovering lost values. Rediscovering lost values. There is something wrong with our world, something fundamentally and basically wrong. I don't think we have to look too far to see that. I'm sure that most of you would agree with me in making that assertion. And when we stop to analyze the cause of our world's ills, many things come to mind. We begin to wonder if it is due to the fact that we don't know enough. But it can't be that. Because in terms of accumulated knowledge we know more today than men have known in any period of human history. We have the facts at our disposal. We know more about mathematics, about science, about social science, and philosophy, than we've ever known in any period of the world's history. So it can't be because we don't know enough.

And then we wonder if it is due to the fact that our sci-

entific genius lags behind. That is, if we have not made enough progress scientifically. Well then, it can't be that. For our scientific progress over the past years has been amazing. Man through his scientific genius has been able to warp distance and place time in chains, so that today it's possible to eat breakfast

in New York City and supper in London, England. I think we have to look much deeper than that if we are to find the real cause of man's problems and the real cause of the world's ills today. If we are to really find it I think we will have to look in the <u>hearts and souls of men.</u> The trouble isn't so much that we don't know enough, but it's as if we aren't good enough. The trouble isn't so much that our scientific genius lags behind, but our moral genius lags behind. The great problem facing modern man is that, that the means by which we live, have outdistanced the spiritual ends for which we live. So we find ourselves caught in a messed-up world. <u>The problem is with man himself and man's soul. We haven't learned how to be just</u> and honest and kind and true and <u>loving. And that is the basis of our problem. The real problem is that through our scientific genius we've made of the world a neighborhood, but through our moral and spiritual genius we've failed to make of it a brotherhood.</u> And the great danger facing us today is not so much the atomic bomb that was created by physical science. Not so much that atomic bomb that you can put in an airplane and drop on the heads of hundreds and thousands of people—as dangerous as that is. <u>But the real danger confronting civilization today is that atomic bomb which lies in the hearts and souls of men, capable of exploding into the vilest of hate and into the most damaging self-ishness. That's the atomic bomb that we've got to fear today. Problem is with the men. Within the heart and the souls of men. That is the real basis of our problem.</u>

My friends, all I'm trying to say is that if we are to go forward today, we've got to go back and rediscover some mighty precious values that we've left behind. That's the only way that we would be able to make of our world a better world, and to make of this world what God wants it to be and the real purpose and meaning of it. The only way we can do it is to go back, and rediscover some mighty precious values that we've left behind.

He continues:

Our situation in the world today reminds me of a very popular situation that took place in the life of Jesus. It was read in the Scripture for the morning, found over in the second chapter of Luke's gospel. The story is very familiar, very popular, we all know it. You remember when Jesus was about twelve years old, there was the custom of the feast. Jesus' parents took him up to Jerusalem. That was an annual occasion, the feast of the Passover, and they went up to Jerusalem and they took Jesus along with them. And they were there a few days, and then after being there they decided to go back home, to Nazareth. And they started out, and I guess as it was the tradition in those days, the father probably traveled in front, and then the mother and the children behind. You see they didn't have the modern conveniences that we have today. They didn't have automobiles and subways and buses. They, they walked, and traveled on donkeys and camels and what have you. So they traveled very slow, but it was usually the tradition for the father to lead the way.

And they left Jerusalem going on back to Nazareth, and I imagine they walked a little while and they didn't look back to see if everybody was there. But then the Scripture says, they went about a day's journey and they stopped, I imagine to check up, to see if everything was all right, and they discovered that something mighty precious was missing. They discovered that Jesus wasn't with them. <u>Jesus wasn't in the midst.</u> And so they, they paused there, and, and looked and they didn't see him around, and they went on, and, and started looking among the kinsfolk, and they went on back to Jerusalem and found him there, in the temple with the doctors of the law.

<u>Now, the real thing that is to be seen here is this, that the parents of Jesus realized that they had left, and that they had lost a mighty precious value.</u> They had sense enough to know that before they could go forward to Nazareth, they had to go backward to Jerusalem <u>to rediscover this value.</u> They knew that. They knew that they couldn't go home to Nazareth until they went back to Jerusalem.

Now that's what we've got to do in our world today. We've left a lot of precious values behind; we've lost a lot of precious values. And if we are to go forward, if we are to make this a better world in which to live, we've got to go back. We've got to rediscover these precious values that we've left behind.

I want to deal with one or two of these mighty precious values that we've left behind, that if we're to go forward and to make this a better world, we must rediscover.

The first is this—the first principle of value that we need to rediscover is this—that all reality hinges on <u>MORAL</u> foundations. In other words, that this is a MORAL universe, and that there are moral laws of the universe, just as abiding as the physical laws. I'm not so sure we all believe that. We, we never doubt that there are physical laws of the universe that we must obey.

But I'm not so sure if we know that there are, are <u>MORAL LAWS</u>, just as abiding as the physical law. I'm not so sure about that. I'm not so sure we really believe that there is a law of love in this universe, and that if you disobey it you'll suffer the consequences. I'm not so sure if we really believe that. Now, at least two things convince me that, that we don't believe that, <u>that we have strayed away from the principle that this is a MORAL UNIVERSE.</u>

The first thing is that we have adopted in the modern world a sort of a relativistic ethic. Now, I'm not trying to use a big word here. I'm trying to say something very concrete. And that is that, that we have accepted the attitude that right and wrong are merely relative to our...

Most people can't stand up for their convictions, because the majority of people might not be doing it. See, everybody's not doing it, so it must be wrong. And, and since everybody is doing it, it must be right. So a sort of numerical interpretation of what's right.

But I'm here to say to you this morning that some things are right and some things are wrong. Eternally so, absolutely so<u>. It's wrong to hate. It always has been wrong and it always will be</u> wrong! <u>It's wrong in America, it's wrong in Germany, it's wrong in Russia, it's wrong in China! It was wrong in two thousand B.C., and it's wrong in nineteen fifty-four A.D.!</u> It <u>always has been wrong, and it always will be wrong!</u>

<u>It's wrong to throw our lives away in riotous living. No matter if everybody in Detroit is doing it. It's wrong! It always will be</u> wrong! <u>And it always has been wrong.</u>

It's wrong in every age, and it's wrong in every nation. *Some things are right and some things are wrong, no matter if everybody is doing the contrary. Some things in this universe are absolute. The God of the universe has made it so. And so long as we adopt this relative attitude toward right and wrong, we're revolting against the very laws of God himself. Now that isn't the only thing that convinces me that we've strayed away from this attitude, this principle. The other thing is that we have adopted a sort of a pragmatic test for right and wrong—whatever works is right. If it works, it's all right. Nothing is wrong but that which does not work. If you don't get caught, it's right. That's the attitude, isn't it? It's all right to disobey the Ten Commandments, but just don't disobey the Eleventh, Thou shall not get caught. That's the attitude. That's the prevailing attitude in, in our culture. No matter what you do, just do it with a, with a bit of finesse. You know, a sort of attitude of the survival of the slickest. Not the Darwinian survival of the fittest, but the survival of the slickest—who, whoever can be the slickest is, is the one who right. It's all right to lie, but lie with dignity. It's all right to steal and to rob and extort, but do it with a bit of finesse.*

It's even all right to hate, but just dress your hate up in the garments of love and make it appear that you are loving when you are actually hating. Just get by! That's the thing that's right according to this new ethic.

My friends, that attitude is destroying the soul of our culture! It's destroying our nation! The thing that we need in the world today, is a group of men and women who will stand up for right and be opposed to wrong, wherever it is. A group of people who have come to see that some things are wrong, whether they're never caught up with. Some things are right, whether nobody sees you doing them or not.

All I'm trying to say is, our world hinges on MORAL FOUNDATIONS. God has made it so! God has made the universe to be based on a MORAL LAW. So long as man disobeys it he is revolting against God. That's what we need in the world today—people who will stand for right and goodness. It's not enough to know the intricacies of zoology and biology. But we must know the intricacies of law. It is not enough to know that two and two makes four. But we've got to know somehow that it's right to be honest and just with our brothers. It's not enough to know all about our philosophical and mathematical disciplines. But we've got to know the simple disciplines, of being honest and loving and just with all humanity. If we don't learn it, we will destroy ourselves, by the misuse of our own powers.

This universe hinges on MORAL FOUNDATIONS. There is something in this universe that justifies Carlyle in saying,

No lie can live forever.

There is something in this universe that justifies the biblical writer in saying, You shall reap what you sow.

This is a law-abiding universe. This is a MORAL UNIVERSE. It hinges on MORAL FOUNDATIONS.

If we are to make of this a better world, we've got to go back and rediscover that precious value that we've left behind. And then there is a second thing, a second principle that we've got to go back and rediscover. And that is that ALL REALITY HAS SPIRITUAL CONTROL. In other words, we've got to go back and rediscover the principle that there is a God behind the process. Well this you say, why is it that you raise that as a point in your sermon, in a church? The mere fact we are at church, we believe in God, we don't need to go back and rediscover that. The mere fact that we are here, and the mere fact that we sing and pray, and come to church—we believe in God. Well, there's some truth in that. But we must remember that it's possible to affirm the existence of God with your lips and deny his existence with your life. The most dangerous type of atheism is not theoretical atheism, but practical atheism— that's the most dangerous type. *And the world, even the church, is filled up with people who pay lip service to God and not life service.* And there is always a danger that we will make it appear externally that we believe in God when internally we don't. We say with our mouths that we believe in Him, but we live with our lives like He never existed. That is the ever-present danger confronting religion. That's a dangerous type of atheism.

And I think, my friends, that that is the thing that has happened in America. *That we have unconsciously left*

God behind. Now, we haven't consciously done it, we, we have unconsciously done it. You see, the text, you remember the text said, that Jesus' parents went a whole day's journey not knowing that he wasn't with them. They didn't consciously leave him behind. It was unconscious. Went a whole day and didn't even know it. It wasn't a conscious process. You see, we didn't grow up and say, now, good-bye God, we're going to leave you now. The materialism in America has been an unconscious thing. Since the rise of the Industrial Revolution in England, and then the invention of all of our gadgets and contrivances and all of the things and modern conveniences—we unconsciously left God behind. We didn't mean to do it.

We just became so involved in, in getting our big bank accounts that we unconsciously forgot about God—we didn't mean to do it. We became so involved in getting our nice luxurious cars, and they're very nice, but we became so involved in it that it became much more convenient to ride out to the beach on Sunday afternoon than to, than to come to church that morning. It, it was an unconscious thing—we didn't mean to do it.

We became so involved and fascinated by the intricacies of television that we found it a little more convenient to stay at home than to come to church. It was an unconscious thing. We didn't mean to do it. We didn't just go up and say, now God, you're gone. We had gone a whole day's journey, and then we came to see that we had unconsciously ushered God out of the universe. A whole day's journey-didn't mean to do it. We just became so involved in things that we forgot about God. And that is the danger confronting us, my friends. That in a nation as ours where we stress mass production, and that's mighty important, where we have so many conveniences and luxuries and all of that, there is the danger that we will unconsciously forget about God. I'm not saying that these things aren't important, we need them, we need cars, we need money, all of that's important to live. But whenever they become substitutes for God, they become injurious.

And may I say to you this morning, that none of these things can ever be real substitutes for God. Automobiles and subways, televisions and radios, dollars and cents, can never be substitutes for God. For long before any of these came into existence, we needed God. And long after they will have passed away, we will still need God.

And I say to you this morning in conclusion that I'm not going to put my ultimate faith in things. I'm not going to put my ultimate faith in gadgets and contrivances. As a young man with most of my life ahead of me, I decided early to give my life to something eternal and absolute. Not to these little gods that are here today and gone tomorrow. But to God who is the same yesterday, today, and forever.

Not in the little gods that can be with us in a few moments of prosperity. But in the God who walks with us through the valley of the shadow of death, and causes us to fear no evil. That's the God.

Not in the god that can give us a few Cadillac cars and Buick convertibles, as nice as they are, that are in style today and out of style three years from now. But the God who threw up the stars, to bedeck the heavens like swinging lanterns of eternity. Not in the god that can throw up a few skyscraping buildings, but the God who threw up the gigantic mountains, kissing the sky, as if to bathe their peaks in the loftitudes. Not in the god that can give us a few televisions and radios, but the God who threw up that great cosmic light, that gets up early in the morning in the eastern horizon, who paints its technicolor across the blue, something that man could never make.

If we are to go forward this morning, we've got to go back and find that God. That is the God that demands and commands our ultimate allegiance.

If we are to go forward, we must go back and rediscover these precious values —that all reality hinges on moral foundations and that all reality has spiritual control. God bless you.

Today's celebrations of Dr. King's legacy have become no more than a novelty. If he were to preach this today he would be called a racist, xenophobe, feminist, homophobe and islamophobe. By those who have and are using the civil rights efforts to gain *special rights* to live an ungodly life. These are an insult to this great Prophet. let's continue speaking on the subject of morality and how it has slowly but surely being taken from us through the political process.

How Would Jesus Vote?

Chapter 2
"ISSUES"
BLACK
AND
WHITE
RACISM

The first of many moral issues that we need to speak of is the issue of race and racism that has dominated the political scene and now more than ever in society as a whole. Most politicians pursue and fill their post only to fulfill desire of their constituents, whether black, white, Hispanic, gay, lesbian, pro-choice, pro-life or other. At this writing, it is reported that in America, there are still too this day former and present members of the Klu Klux Klan, Muslim Brotherhood and other hate groups who have been notorious in their display of hatred and bigotry toward any other race different than their own. I'm sure this can be found in other nations as well, and guess what, all in the name of God. Morality, yea right. If God is love and we know that He is, how can we continue to vote for those men and women who hate in the name of God. We allow them to make decisions that affect our lives in this nation and throughout the world.

Morality deals with doing that which is right based on the word of God. Nowhere in the scripture do we find it right or proper to hate another person because of the color of their skin. The believer's absence of involvement in the governmental (political) sphere of influence is to be blamed for the many ungodly things that are being legislated as acceptable behavior. Christians must get involved not just vote but become the person who is seeking to be voted for. Who can better legislate that which is right and proper based on the word of God better than someone who knows God and knows His voice, it doesn't matter if the candidates are of a different race or gender. In light of the present atmosphere in many Christians nations, racism is sure to be displayed in the great way during elections.

Due to the prevalence of racism throughout the world, there is usually a lack of presence in the many races living in that nation. For instance, in countries like South Africa, there would be mostly Whites trying to gain the leadership position. Whenever someone other than a white person sought election racism would rear its ugly head. I am convinced that any African American candidate whether Presidential or other, *would be considered the savior of their race* that they have been looking for a very long time; forgetting that there is only one savior and his name is Jesus Christ. He didn't just save one race of people but he became the savior of the whole ***human race***. Not only did he become the savior of all, but he also became responsible for all mankind.

Because there has been little or no ethnic diversity represented throughout each level of government in America and others, it would be easy to vote for such a person who can be identified as "one of us." You could expect the nonbeliever to respond is such a manner but not the mature believer. The believer has the advantage of **knowing**. This knowing is not based on the obvious but this knowing is obtained in the prayer closet. As a result of this kind of thinking, many black, and white Christians will cast a vote for a candidate just because of his or her race. Again, this book is written to Christians; those who say that they are followers of Jesus Christ. God never told you that some man or woman was your source for a fulfilled life. God is the only source of a fulfilled life and Jesus came to give all mankind that kind of life. Life and it more abundantly. (John 10:10) As a Christian, you cannot vote for a candidate just because of race, gender or political allegiance.

This book is being written to give a wake-up call to the body of Christ that we have a Godly responsibility to involve ourselves in the political process and cast a vote that has been given to us while we are in a place of consecration concerning this matter. In other words, we should seek the face of God for the purpose of finding God's mind on the situation. Jeremiah said that if we seek God with all our hearts, we would find him. God doesn't look at the race or gender, nor the political party of the candidate. God looks at the HEART. (I Samuel 16:7)

Now, this is significant because if Christians pursue the political process as those who are not Christians, we will most likely make the irrevocable mistake of putting power into the hands of those who will attempt and most likely succeed in legislating everything they can that is against God, you can see it today. This is why we must hear God's voice in the matter. Only God knows the heart of a man. Only He knows whether or not he can turn that heart to do His will. God knows the heart of all candidates and those to come, after all he created them. No one race of people is inherently evil therefore we must know the heart of God concerning each of the candidates. King Solomon declared that the king's heart is in the Lords hand and He turns it wherever he desires (Proverbs 21:1).

Some elections do not present on the surface an overwhelming favorite for the Christian and for this reason, we must do our due diligence to hear God's voice and obey it. What do you do when each of the candidates has some real issues when you put them and their values up against the word of God? It becomes a necessity that Christians everywhere unite in an effort of prayer and fasting, so that we may know who to cast the vote for. Only God knows. How would Jesus Vote?

As a matter of fact, when Moses was the leader of Israel, he had been given the responsibility to bring the children of Israel out of Egyptian bondage and take them into the land that God had promised would be theirs some four hundred years earlier. Moses had an older brother and sister, Aaron and Miriam. Moses had married a woman of a different race (a black woman). His brother and sister didn't like it and spoke against his marriage. The Bible declares that because of this, God made Moses' sister Miriam become leprous-white as snow. In other words, there were immediate consequences to her for having a racist heart. Although Moses' wife was a black woman, God did not punish him for marrying her. On the contrary, he celebrated his marriage to this woman. *This is clearly seen in how quickly God judged the situation. God judged the hatred that was in Aaron and Miriam's heart, not the interracial marriage*.

> *Numbers* 12: 1 *And Miriam and Aaron spake against Moses because of the Ethiopian woman whom he had married: for he had married an Ethiopian woman. NU* 12:2 *And they said, Hath the LORD indeed spoken only by Moses? hath he not spoken also by us? And the LORD heard it. NU* 12:3 *(Now the man Moses was very meek, above all the men which were upon*

the face of the earth.) NU 12:4 *And the LORD spake suddenly unto Moses, and unto Aaron, and unto
Miriam, Come out ye three unto the tabernacle of
the congregation. And they three came out. NU* 12:5
*And the LORD came down in the pillar of the cloud,
and stood in the door of the tabernacle, and called
Aaron and Miriam: and they both came forth. NU
12:6 And He said, hear now my words: If there be
a prophet among you, I the LORD will make myself
known unto him in a vision, and will speak unto him
in a dream. NU* 12:7 *My servant Moses is not so, who
is faithful in all mine house. NU* 12:8 *With him will
I speak mouth to mouth, even apparently, and not in
dark speeches; and the similitude of the LORD shall
he behold: wherefore then were ye not afraid to speak
against my servant Moses? NU* 12:9 *And the anger of
the LORD was kindled against them; and he departed.
NU* 12:10 *And the cloud departed from off the tabernacle; and, behold, Miriam became leprous, white as
snow: and Aaron looked upon Miriam, and, behold,
she was leprous. NU* 12:11 *And Aaron said unto Moses, Alas, my lord, I beseech thee, lay not the sin upon
us, wherein we have done foolishly, and wherein we
have sinned. NU* 12:12 *Let her not be as one dead, of
whom the flesh is half consumed when he cometh out
of his mother's womb.*

Verse 11 called this act sin. There is no black
and white in God. The apostle Paul put it like this
in the book of Galatians 3:28: *There is neither Jew nor
Greek, there is neither bond nor free, there is neither male
nor female: for ye are all one in Christ Jesus.* God does not
have respect of persons and neither, should we. All
human beings came from one man and one woman
Adam and Eve.

Another case found in the New Testament
deals with a Chief Apostle named Peter. He is the
disciple that had the great revelation (we will dis-

cuss how important having a revelation is later) concerning Jesus as the Son of God. He's the same Peter who walked on the water and finally the Peter who got his taxes paid by catching a fish and finding money in his mouth. This same Peter along with some of the other disciples had a racist heart and attitude. God loved Peter and gave him the opportunity to change his views, but initially, he did not. Let's take a look at the scriptural account found in the book of Acts chapters ten and eleven. The entire chapter is necessary to read so that you can get a real sense of what's happening.

Acts *10:1 There was a certain man in Caesarea called Cornelius, a centurion of the band called the Italian band, 10:2 A devout man, and one that feared God with all his house, which gave much alms to the people, and prayed to God alway.* **10:3 He saw** *in a vision evidently about the ninth hour of the of the day an angel of God coming in to him, and saying unto him, Cornelius 10:4 And when he looked on him, he was afraid, and I said. What is it, Lord? And he said unto him, Thy prayers and thine alms are come up for a memorial before God. 10:5 And now send men to Joppa, and call for one Simon, whose surname is Peter: 10:6 He lodgeth with one Simon a tanner, whose house is by the sea side: he shall tell thee what thou oughtest to do. 10: 7 And when the angel which spake unto Cornelius was departed, he called two of his household servants, and a devout soldier of them that waited on him continually; 10:8 And when he had declared all these things unto them, he sent them to Joppa. 10:9 On the morrow, as they went on their journey, and drew nigh unto the city, Peter went up upon the housetop to pray about the sixth hour: 10: 1 0 And he became very hungry, and would have eaten: but while they made ready, he fell into a trance, 10:11 And saw heaven opened, and a certain vessel descending unto him, as it had been a great sheet knit at the four corners, and let down to the earth: 10:12 Wherein were all manner of four-footed beasts of the earth, and wild beasts, and creeping things, and fowls of the air. 10:13 And there came a voice to him, Rise,*

Peter; kill, and eat 10: 14 But Peter said, Not so, Lord; for I have never eaten anything that is common or unclean. 10: 15 And the voice spake unto him again the second time, What God hath cleansed, that call not thou common. 10: 16 This was done thrice: and the vessel was received up again into heaven 10: 17 Now while Peter doubted in himself what this vision which he had seen should mean, behold, the men which were sent from Cornelius had made inquiry for Simon's house, and stood before the gate, 10: 18 And called, and asked whether Simon, which was surnamed Peter, were lodged there. 10: 19 While Peter thought on the vision, the Spirit said unto him, Behold, three men seek thee. 10:20 Arise therefore, and get thee down, and go with them, doubting nothing: for I have sent them. 10:21 Then Peter went down to the men which were sent unto him from Cornelius; and said, Behold, I am he whom ye seek: what is the cause wherefore ye are come? 10:22 And they said, Cornelius the centurion, a just man, and one that feareth God, and of good report among all the nation of the Jews, was warned from God by an holy angel to send for thee into his house, and to hear words of thee. 10:23 Then called he them in, and lodged them. And on the morrow Peter went away with them, and certain brethren from Joppa accompanied him. 10:24 And the morrow after they entered into Caesarea. And Cornelius waited for them, and had called together his kinsmen and near friends. 10:25 And as Peter was coming in, Cornelius met him, and fell down at his feet, and worshipped him. 10:26 But Peter took him up, saying, Stand up; I myself also am a man. 10:27 And as he talked with him, he went in, and found many that were come together. 10:28 And he said unto them, Ye know how that it is an unlawful thing for a man that is a Jew to keep company, or come unto one of another nation; but God hath showed me that I should not call any man common or unclean. 10:29 Therefore came I unto you without gainsaying, as soon as I was sent for: I ask therefore for what intent ye have sent for me? 10:30 And Cornelius said, four days ago I was fasting until this hour; and at the ninth hour I prayed in my house, and, behold, a man stood before me in bright clothing, 10:31 And said, Cornelius, thy prayer is heard, and thine alms are had in remembrance in the sight of God

10:32 Send therefore to Joppa, and call hither Simon, whose surname is Peter; he is lodged in the house of one Simon a tanner by the sea side: who, when he cometh, shall speak unto thee. 10:33 Immediately therefore I sent to thee; and thou hast well done that thou art come. Now therefore are we all here present before God, to hear all things that are commanded thee of God 10:34 Then Peter opened his mouth, and said, of a truth I perceive that God is no respecter of persons 10:35 But in every nation he that feareth him, and worketh righteousness, is accepted with him. 10:36 The word which God sent unto the children of Israel, preaching peace by Jesus Christ: (he is Lord of all.) 10:37 That word, I say, ye know, which was published throughout all Judaea, and began from Galilee, after the baptism which John preached;10:38 How God anointed Jesus of Nazareth with the Holy Ghost and with power: who went about doing good, and healing all that were oppressed of the devil; for God was with him 10:39 And we are witnesses of all things which he did both in the land of the Jews, and in Jerusalem; whom they slew and hanged on a tree: 10:40 Him God raised up the third day, and showed him openly; 10:41 Not to all the people, but unto witnesses chosen before of God, even to us, who did eat and drink with him after he rose from the dead 10: 42 And he commanded us to preach unto the people, and to testify that it is he which was ordained of God to be the Judge of quick and dead 10:43 To him give all the prophets witness, that through his name whosoever believeth in him shall receive remission of sins. 10:44 While Peter yet spake these words, the Holy Ghost fell on all them which heard the word 10:45 And they of the circumcision which believed were astonished, as many as came with Peter, because that on the Gentiles also was poured out the gift of the Holy Ghost. 10:46 For they heard them speak with tongues, and magnify God Then answered Peter, 10:47 Can any man forbid water, that these should not be baptized, which have received the Holy Ghost as well as we? 10:48 And he commanded them to be baptized in the name of the Lord Then prayed they him to tarry certain days.

I'm aware that the chapter is lengthy but as I

mentioned, it is necessary so that you can get a sense of what is actually transpiring. I will summarize what happened in chapter ten and chapters eleven as well because chapter ten and eleven go together.

Please take the time to read chapter eleven for yourself. Peter is busy about the Lord's work doing what he could to fulfill what the Lord Jesus had commanded him upon His going back to heaven. While taking an afternoon nap and waiting for his meals to be prepared, he fell into a trance. In the trance, there is a sheet let down from heaven from one corner of the earth to the other and within this sheet there appeared some wild animals that were unlawful for Jews to eat. But a voice cries out to him to kill and eat. Peter's response was a denial of the commandment. He gives the reason for his denial by justifying he had never eaten anything common or unclean. It was against the Jewish culture to do such a thing. (It was against Jewish culture to love another race of people other than their own). The Lord responded by saying, "nothing that I have cleaned is common or unclean." This happened three times and after the third, time Peter began to be in great thought as to what this might mean. While he was pondering and trying to figure it all out, God had sent the answer. A knock at the door where Peter was staying interrupted his meditation. Those at the door were sent from a **Gentile** man named Cornelius who loved God but was of **another race**. He also had a vision, but in his vision the Lord instructed Cornelius (the gentile man, "Black Man) to call for Peter (the Jew "White Man") so that he could show him what to do to get born again and filled with the Holy Spirit. The Lord instructed Peter to go with the men and not to *doubt* that He sent them.

When Peter arrived at Cornelius's house he found it filled Cornelius' family and friends who were Gentiles like him. They were in great anticipation of what God was going to do for them, a people of another race other than Jews. Peter begins to explain to Cornelius how it is unlawful for Jews (White People) to keep company with people of other races (Black People), but then he said, "**God showed me** (Revelation) that I should not *call any man common* or *unclean.*" After Cornelius explains to Peter the vision that he had, *Peter exclaims that his perception is now that **God is no respecter of persons** but in any nation (**race**) he that fears God and works righteousness is accepted with God.* The chapter ends with the Gentiles receiving salvation and the baptism in the Holy Spirit.

Chapter eleven begins with the news of the Gentiles receiving salvation, but what should have been a joyous occasion turned out to be the opposite. Those who were still of the persuasion that their race was the only legitimate race contended with Peter as to why he would do such a thing. Peter rehearses the events in their ears and the Bible says that they held their peace and rejoiced that the Lord had granted Salvation to the Gentiles as well as the Jews. It's wonderful that the church finally got it or did they?

Here is Peter who had the revelation that Jesus was the Son of God and know that God is no respect of persons was still struggling with racism because of peer pressure. This will give us some insight into dealing with this ever-present problem. A problem that could have and should have been dealt with many years ago, but because the **prominent church leaders** in those years did not deal with it, it is has become much bigger now.

In the book of Galatians the Apostle Paul took issue with the Apostle Peter for His racist ways. Here's the scriptural account of it.

GA 2: 11 *But when Peter was come to Antioch, I withstood him to the face, because he was to be blamed. GA* 2: 12 *For before that certain came from James, he did eat with the Gentiles: but when they were come, he withdrew and separated himself, fearing them which were of the circumcision. GA* 2: 13 *And the other Jews dissembled likewise with him' insomuch that Barnabas also was carried away with their' dissimulation. GA* 2: 14 *But when I saw that they walked not uprightly according to the truth of the gospel, I said unto Peter before them all, If thou, being a Jew, livest after the manner of Gentiles, and not as do the Jews, why compellest thou the Gentiles to live as do the Jews?*

Peter was like many of our modern-day preachers, he'd hang out with the Gentiles as long as there were no Jews of renown around but as soon as they came around he would leave and act like he didn't even know the people he had just been talking to. The Apostle Paul said I withstood him to his face concerning his racism and placed the blame for the gap in the relationship or (brotherhood) on him.

I'm going to be like the Apostle Paul and place blame squarely on the shoulders to whom I believe it belongs as it relates to racism today. I am convinced that when preachers had a place of influence in the America years ago, if they would have stood in their pulpits and preached the real gospel of Jesus Christ, racism would have never gotten the strangled hold that it has today. I believe there are two reasons for this, there could be more but these two I'm sure of.

The first one is obvious and it is this: many of those preachers and church leaders were racist themselves even members of hate groups such as the KKK and others. So, they could not preach the real gospel. They may have been kicked out of their "fraternity". How can any man or woman who calls themselves a believer in Jesus have hatred in his or her heart toward another race? In 1 John, he said if any man hated his brother he is a _**murderer**_ and you know that no murderer has eternal life dwelling in him. I can't imagine the judgment that is awaiting those who use the sacred desk to perpetuate a gospel of hatred, separation and a gospel other than that which Jesus and the Apostles preached, which was the gospel of love, forgiveness, and fellowship.

The second is not as obvious as the first but I pray the light of the truth will make it obvious to all. Many pastors and ministers who may have not been racist but did not preach against racism to their congregations was because they were afraid that they would lose their livelihood. Many were afraid, which is evidenced in Dr. King's letter from a Birmingham jail. Where he wondered where were the white clergy coming to his aid. This is still true today just as much as it was then, they fear they would turn off their big donors (many of whom are racist) and if the pastor speaks against racism, it could have jeopardized the lavished lifestyles they had come to enjoy. These actually traded the truth that is designed to set men free, for trinkets of treason. What a travesty and tragedy.

The pulpit is the place to proclaim the truth. Jesus said that "you shall know the truth and the truth will make you free. If you were a racist before you got born again, you're in all likelihood still a racist or have some racist values. Without the gospel truth about racism being preached to you and you listen, you are not able to have a change in your heart. According to John 16, The Holy Spirit is The Spirit of Truth that causes conviction in the hearts of men. When any man (regardless of his skin color) is deprived of the truth on any matter they will remain in that same old traditional demonic dark place. There are pulpits today that are still withholding truth about racism from the people that they are responsible for. This could be call quenching the spirit. The Apostle John said that he had no greater joy than that his children walk in truth, **3 John 1:4**. Racism is a sin and an abomination to the God who created all men in His own Image and Likeness. It is very important that we who are a part of Christ's body be guiltless of voting for a person because they are of the same race or gender that we are. Remember that God is our source, not the government.

Here's my experience as a pastor with racism in the church. I was a member of a particular church back in the eighties that was pastored by a white man who had moved from California to assume the pastorate. I was going through quite a bit of difficulty in my marriage and life at that time. Not having many believers in my immediate family left me with no one to agree with me in prayer or offer council or godly advice. I spent quite a bit of time talking to phone counselors. I was tremendously blessed on many occasions through those phone calls and I felt that a local ministry such as this would be beneficial here. I approached the pastor with the idea to which he flat out rejected, until a few weeks later he was contacted by one of the phone ministries that I had frequently called. They asked him about the prospect of putting a prayer call center here and he accepted. This was the first time that I had seen racism and recognized it.

As a pastor, through the years we have had several white people come and visit our church and many have joined only to leave after usually a short period of time. I got born again in 1981 and spent the vast majority of my developmental years as a Christian under white leadership. I had no problem submitting to the leadership because my service and submission was unto God and not the man. Many of those who left, left because of peer pressure from family and friends. God sets the members in His body as it pleases Him but we allow racism to thwart God's plan for the local church.

How would Jesus Vote?

Chapter 3
PRO-CHOICE (DEATH) OR PRO-LIFE

The second issue of morality is that of abortion (murder of the unborn), which is the politically correct way of saying murder. In the so-called great Christian nation America, in 1970, a lawsuit was filed in a Texas courthouse by an unmarried woman who already had two children and was pregnant with her third attempt to gain the right to play God and have an abortion. Established many years prior by those who had morals, *a sense of what was right and proper,* completely based on the word of the Lord, abortions were illegal throughout the nation unless in the event that it was medically necessary to save the mother's life. The decision to make the murder of the unborn illegal was based on the knowledge found in the Bible and not from some theory. This proves that the argument of those who say that a woman has a right to choose to murder the unborn baby is unfounded and in direct contradiction to God's order and is outright demonic.

What she was trying to do was to get rid of the consequence of the **choice** she made to have sex outside of marriage. The bible calls this fornication, another violation in the order of God. Any sexual act outside of the marriage covenant is sin. Her promiscuous lifestyle had previously yielded two children and the one she was seeking to get permission to murder. This pregnant and soon to be the mother of three was given the name Roe, I suppose an attempt to conceal her identity. The district attorney in the case was named Wade, which is where the famed Roe VS Wade case came about. This case went from court to court until it made its way to the Supreme Court the highest court in the land. In 1973 the supreme court of America *chose* to go against what had already been *accepted as right and proper.* They deemed it the *legal* right of a woman to have the *choice* whether to give birth to her child or murder it, presently known as the pro-choice movement or a woman's right to choose murder as a form of birth control.

The battle rages on in the courts over this issue. The church's passive nature and in particular the black church again made it possible for the passing of this law and many others like it. Some sitting on the benches of the Supreme Court are those who oppose God and everything that represents God. t's as if they are there to impose the will of Satan in a nation founded on many of the principles found throughout the Bible. Those Supreme Court justices and politicians were put into those positions and given judicial and legislative authority to adjudicate and legislate sin and unrighteousness because the church did not do and up to this point does not do its job.

Your government actually put within the hands of one who had no choice nor the ability to choose according to the bible whether the child would experience life outside his or her mother's womb. As a result of this, all those women who were either pregnant or soon to be pregnant had been given the legal right to play the role of creator. Got real problems with this assertion? Here's why. Throughout The Bible it is made clear who the author of life and the giver of choice is. Yes, it is God. The one who created all things including you and me. If God wanted me murdered in my mother's womb, why did he allow me to be conceived?

The number of babies that have been murdered in America since this ruling would astound even the murderer if they would dare look at them. I know the use of the word murder in the place of abortion is not politically correct, but if you haven't figured that out yet, I have no interest in being politically correct, but being morally right. Moses spoke in Deut. 30:19:

I call heaven and earth to record this day against you, that I have set before you life and death, blessing and cursing: <u>therefore choose life</u>, that both thou and thy seed may live.

It is clear that the giver of life is God. In other words, if you didn't give life, then you don't have the *right* of *choice* to take the life. All life is given by God. Only He is the giver of life. The only real choice is life. Part of the argument that helped legalize abortion was the talk of the baby itself. They say that it's not a life but it is just a piece of flesh commonly referred to as a fetus. They also allege that since it is just a piece of flesh, the fetus doesn't experience any pain while it's being murdered. (torn apart or having it brains sucked out while still alive). Just think how absurd, inhumane and barbaric this is. If you have a hangnail it causes excruciating pain, think about having your arms or legs pulled from your body while conscious.

Let's take another look into the Bible and see what the author of life has to say about this so-called piece of flesh that has no life and feels no pain.

David says in Ps *104:30: Thou sendest forth thy Spirit, they are created.* As soon as the sperm and the egg come together, a living being full of life (spirit) has just been <u>created</u>.

Job said in chapter 33:4 *The spirit of God hath made me, and the breath of the Almighty hath given me life.* It's clear again that God is the creator and the giver of life. Due to our humanistic views, our understanding of the human makeup has left us. Man is a tripartite being. This simply means that he has three components to his make up: these are the Spirit, the Soul, and the Body.

The components explained: The SPIRIT is the very core of man, Gen, 1: 26 God made man in His own image and after His likeness. If mankind is made in the image of God then man has to be a spirit just like God. Remember David said that God sends His spirit and they are created. God himself lives in our spirits and Spirits don't die. They live forever.

The SOUL is comprised of the mind, will, emotions, intellect, and imagination. The soul has been defined as the seat of the emotions and the place of feelings and also, the heart, not the human heart. Proverbs 23:7 says, as he thinketh in his heart so is he. You don't think in your physical heart but you think in your mind. The soul was designed by God to be under the control of the man's spirit which is to be controlled by God's spirit (the Holy Spirit), always having His thoughts, will, feelings, intelligence and His imagination in line with God. When Adam and Eve sinned against God their spirit lost control of their soul and because of this, God lost control of their spirit. The Bible says that when man died, he died spiritually. This is crucially important to understand.

The BODY is where the Spirit and Soul live, simply put, the body is the house for both the spirit and soul, also called in the Bible the flesh.

The Fallen man left without the source of life and that which is right, began to devise his own way of life. This lifestyle eventually prompted God to change his mind about the creation of mankind. He decided to destroy what sin had accomplished in men's flesh. All mankind was destroyed except Noah, his wife, his three sons, and their wives. Noah had evidently maintained a sense of control of his being so much so that he found grace in God's eyes and because of this God spared mankind.

As you can see the man is more than just a body or a piece of flesh. He is a unique being that has characteristics resembling the creator. King David said in Psalms 139:13-16, *13 For thou hast possessed my reins: thou hast covered me in my mother's womb.14 I will praise thee; for I am fearfully and wonderfully made: marvellous are thy works; and that my soul knoweth right well.15 My substance was not hid from thee, when I was made in secret, and curiously wrought in the lowest parts of the earth.16 Thine eyes did see my substance, yet being unperfect; and in thy book all my members were written, which in continuance were fashioned, when as yet there was none of them.*

How dare we stand so bold to declare that the human life found within the womb is like cancer and must be removed at any cost?

How would Jesus Vote?

Chapter 4
PLANNED (KLANNED) PARENTHOOD

I introduce to you Ms. Margaret Sanger whose efforts for Planned Parenthood has evolved into a gigantic monster that has provided abortion services and has murdered millions of babies since 1973. Read this alarming information which really describes this woman's motive. Not only was she a racist, but she effectively put into place a strategic plan to minimize the African American race by offering abortions to many unsuspecting victims carrying out her murderous plot. These quotes truly show the intent of this demonized woman's heart who is praised by many, including blacks, as a champion of women's causes.

Margaret Sanger, the alcoholic and Demerol addict, who spawned the International Planned Parenthood Federation, was a proponent of forced eugenics, segregation, abortion, birth control, and sexual immorality. Here are some of her quotes.

> *"The most merciful thing that a family does to one of its infant members is to kill it." "Birth control must lead ultimately to a cleaner race." "We should hire three or four colored ministers, preferably with social-service backgrounds, and with engaging personalities. The most successful educational approach to the Negro is through a religious appeal. We don't want the word to go out that we want to exterminate the Negro population" "Eugenic sterilization is an urgent need ...*
>
> *We must prevent multiplication of this bad stock."*
>
> *"Eugenics is the most adequate and thorough avenue to the solution of **racial, political and social problems.**

"Birth control itself often denounced as a violation of natural law, is nothing more or less than the facilitation of the process of weeding out the unfit, of preventing the birth of defectives or of those who will become defectives."

"The unbalance between the birth rate of the 'unfit' and the 'fit,' [is] the greatest present menace to civilization ... the most urgent problem today is how to limit and discourage the over-fertility of the mentally and physically defective."

"The campaign for birth control is not merely of eugenic value but is practically identical with the final aims of eugenics."

"Our failure to segregate morons who are increasing and multiplying ... a deadweight of human waste ... an ever-increasing, unceasingly spawning class of human beings who never should have been born at all."

"The undeniably feeble-minded should, indeed, not only be discouraged but prevented _from propagating their kind._"

"The procreation of [the diseased, the feeble-minded and paupers] should be stopped." "The marriage bed is the most degenerative influence in the social order ..."

"[Our objective is] unlimited sexual gratification without the burden of unwanted children ..."

"[Mandatory] sterilization for [the insane and feeble-minded] is the answer."

"Give dysgenic groups [people with 'bad genes'] in our population their choice of segregation or [compulsory] sterilization."

Margaret Sanger, Founder of Planned Parenthood proposed the American Baby Code that states, *"No woman shall have the legal right to bear a child ... without a permit for parenthood"*. Margaret Sanger, Founder of Planned Parenthood, proposed the Population Congress with the aim,

"...to give certain dysgenic groups in our population their choice of segregation or sterilization.

This organization has nothing to do with planning parenthood but rather promoting sexual promiscuity and everything that God declared sinful. **Fornication** in every age sector (sex without being legally marriage), **Adultery** (married but having sex with someone other than the spouse). **Homosexuality** (sex between same-sex partners). **Bestiality** (sex between humans and animals). If by chance any one of the participants happens to get pregnant while practicing, they were afforded the murdering services of PLANNED PARENTHOOD to dispose of their consequences.

Here are some startling statistics that are directly related to the, as one person called it, "Klan Parenthood". The inference, of course, is of that of the KKK, those who sought to destroy every human being that did not look like a member of the supreme race. Those who sought to destroy every human being that did not look like them at any cost. Their efforts were meted out on blacks
for many years and it still continues. What Planned parenthood has done is to effort to kill that So and So before it gets here.

Culture of Life Foundation & Institute -As data from the 2001 census were released this past

March, demographers expressed surprise that the Hispanic population had already supplanted African-Americans as our nation's largest minority. The trends had pointed in that direction for the last decade, but the experts had predicted that Hispanics would not actually take the lead until around 2005. But the census revealed that in fact, it was in 2000 that the Hispanic population exceeded that of blacks.

Why is the number of Hispanics growing so much faster than the number of blacks? The reasons are many and complex; beyond the obvious cause of immigration, we can only surmise about how such factors as family unity, economic opportunity, crime, addiction, and education affect individual decisions to bring children into the world. But one cause is clear: because black women have undergone a disproportionate number of abortions in the twenty-eight years since *Roe v. Wade,* millions of black children and young adults are not present to be counted in the census.

These numbers are shocking. African-American women constitute 13.5 of the U.S. female population but they undergo 34% of all the abortions in this country. Their abortion rate (31 per 1,000 women) is approximately 2.6 times the rate for white women (12 per 1,000). The abortion industry reports very few statistics and strongly resists any effort at reporting more, so we must estimate further conclusions: African-American pro-life activists estimate that about 1,400 black babies have died in abortions, on average, each day since abortion was mandated a constitutional right. That makes 546,000 killed per year, or about 24 million people at this writing since *Roe vs. Wade.*

Abortion also impacts the survivors: the women who undergo an abortion, the men who are confirmed by abortion in the evasion of their responsibilities, and the community which is in the throes of a culture of death. Ten out of eleven studies of American women show there is a link between abortion and breast cancer, so it is not surprising that African- American women suffer breast cancer at a greater rate. From 1975 to 1990, breast cancer mortality in young black women increased by over 12%, while the rate for white women was declining by about 9%, over the same period. Young black women have abortions at a greater rate than young white women, and abortion at an early age further increases the breast cancer risk giving the increased rate of abortions among African-Americans, it is fair to ask whether this community is specifically targeted by the abortion industry. The writings of Margaret Sanger, the founder of Planned Parenthood, given ample evidence of her belief in eugenics and her plan to reduce the African-American population through "family planning". But that was over sixty years ago. Today, however, we do see a concentration of abortion businesses in African-American neighborhoods. For example, according to Michigan Right to Life, of the 36 abortion clinics remaining in Michigan, eleven are in Detroit, a black-majority city. Of those eleven, nine are in African-American neighborhoods or have predominantly African-American customers

When we recall that almost all the present African- American representatives in Congress favor abortion, we conclude we are faced with an astounding voluntary surrender of power. When we add the impact of abortion on the living and the disproportionate effect within the African-American community, the ironic tragedy of the "pro-choice" position of black leadership becomes even more obvious.

For the sake of our nation and our Afri-can-American brothers and sisters, we must pray that a black leader will arise who will defend the lives and health of his or her people against the forces that uses death to shape society to their liking.

What's more troubling is the absence of the black clergy who are willing to defend the black baby from this racist motivated plot to destroy the black race. This quote from earlier speaks volumes "Eugenics is the most adequate and thorough avenue to the solution of ***racial, political and social problems. Politicize the racial and social problems and black clergy won't get involved.*** This has to change if these babies are going to have a chance to live.

I'm not suggesting that African American babies are the only babies being murdered but the despairing differences comparatively speaking will make any person who understands how valuable life is, cringe. As I mentioned, the statistics are overwhelming. There are a large number of African American politicians who favor the murder of the unborn. Which means they actually cast votes to keep abortions legal and to further remove any lingering issues concerning abortions. And I would assume that many of these figure heads call themselves the big C word, Christians. How can you be a Christian and you know the will of God and cast a vote to legalize or uphold the murder of innocent life? I am sure that there are those in other nations who will have similar statistics.

America needs to Wake up, there are those pursuing seats in government all over this nation of ours who are making their agreement known to what is happening by their votes to keep legal the murder of the unborn and of course other things as well. Regardless of race, gender or political allegiance, Jesus came to give us life by giving up his life. For the murdered unborn, what life were they afforded by the sacrifice of the life of Jesus?

Thousands of blacks were ruthlessly targeted for the purpose of extinction. The days of physical lynching have been minimized tremendously but another form of lynching was in the works by such strategist as Margaret Sanger and others like her. Their strategy to use *death to shape society to their liking has* produced even greater results. At least 20 to 25 million African American babies have been lynched while in their mother's womb thanks to Planned Parenthood and others.

In America today, almost as many African-American children are aborted as are born. A black baby is three times more likely to be murdered in the womb than a white baby. Since 1973, abortion has reduced the black population by over 25 percent. Twice as many African-Americans have died from abortion than have died from AIDS, accidents, violent crimes, cancer, and heart disease combined. Every three days, more African-Americans are killed by abortion than have been killed by the Ku Klux Klan in its entire history.

Planned Parenthood operates the nation's largest chain of abortion clinics and almost 80 percent of its facilities are located in minority neighborhoods. About 13 percent of American women are black, but they submit to over 35 percent of the abortions.

Did you know that Planned Parenthood is the number one provider of abortions in America? Yes, number one. And Planned Parenthood is making quite a lot of money off this dirty business of killing unborn children. In fact, they reported $114.8 million in profit during their last fiscal year. That's quite a lot of profit for an organization that calls themselves a non-profit. Meanwhile, American taxpayers, like you and me, kicked in more than $550 million worth of government grants and contracts at both the state and federal levels for Planned Parenthood. That's right. Thanks to your tax dollars, Planned Parenthood is a very profitable "non-profit."

The profitability of the abortion industry has grown in recent years with the use of the aborted baby parts being used in all sorts of consumable products, makeup and stem cell research. The profit does not end.

This is the 21st century lynching, it's called the Partial Birth Abortion.

Partial Birth Abortion 1

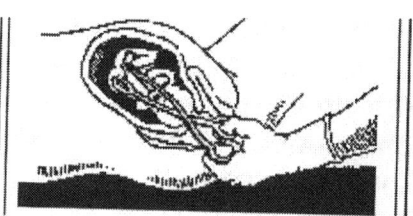 Guided by ultrasound, the abortionist grabs the baby's leg with forceps.

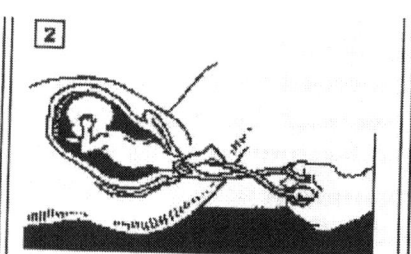

The baby's leg is pulled out into the birth canal

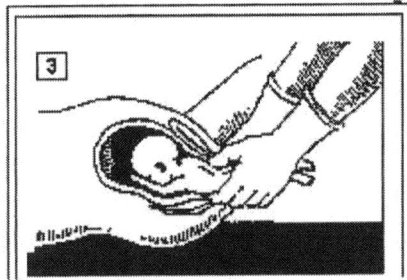 The abortionist delivers the baby's entire body, except for the head.

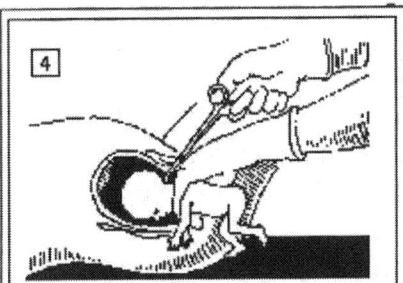 The abortionist jams scissor into the baby's skull. The scissors are then opened to enlarge the hole.

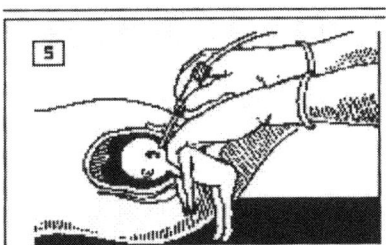 The scissors are removed and a suction tube is inserted. The child's brains are rocked out causing: the skull to collapse. The dead baby is then removed.

Notice that the well paid practitioner/ murderer places his hand around the neck of the baby making sure that the head doesn't come out of the womb while he does the unthinkable.

This depicts such a clear picture of the attempt of the black man's oppressors to do what they can to keep him from thinking independently or thinking for himself. With the noose around the neck, airflow to the brain is cut off and eventually, death ensues... This is so ironic because the advocates of partial-birth abortions want you to have a choice of whether to murder your unborn child but do everything to prevent you from choosing to think for yourself.

Margaret Sanger's agenda has expanded into Infanticide, the killing of the newborn. It has often been interpreted as a primitive method of birth control and a means of ridding a group of its weak and deformed children, but most societies actively desire children and put them to death (or allow them to die) only under exceptional circumstances. Many states are legalizing this type of murder of babies while protecting "animals".

WHAT A PLOT.

This information may offend some because of its brashness and some may feel that if I were to be politically correct I would not print such information like this. This is where we are as a nation.

How would Jesus Vote?

Chapter 5
LGBTQ &
THE SANCTITY OF
MARRIAGE

In the case of marriage. Some very confused, deceived, misinformed or *however they are to be described people*, who refuse to use the Bible to validate their gender have convinced and are convincing people throughout this nation and the world that it is right and acceptable for two people of the same sex to enter into the covenant relationship of marriage. We have practicing homosexuals in positions of power in those spheres of influence that we mentioned earlier and the others that we didn't, who are using their influence and power to legislate a lifestyle that God Himself called an abomination and destroyed what had become a cultural norm in the towns of Sodom and Gomorrah in the Bible (Genesis 19:1-25).

Some preachers have said that God did not destroy the cities of Sodom and Gomorrah because of homosexuality. They say that God destroyed the cities of Sodom and Gomorrah because He could not find 10 righteous people in them. But they fail to acknowledge the fact that God came to Abraham and informed him of his intentions to destroy the cities of Sodom and Gomorrah because of their homosexual practices. Taking the scriptures out of context to be politically correct or socially acceptable is an abomination in and of itself.

There is a direct attack on the institution of marriage. Marriage according to the model government found throughout the word of God is between one man and one woman. Not between two men or two women. Marriage is defined as "The unity of man and women, as implied in her being formed out of man," not some politically correct terms of *Same-Sex Marriage, Civil Unions* or *Domestic Partnerships*. Through the political process, there are states that have legalized the union between two persons of the same-sex and there are others who are desiring to do the same. The arguments of those who choose to live this *lifestyle* are that it is their right to choose their sexual orientation. How do you choose how you are created biologically?

Historically, marriage is the first institution set up by God and it is the oldest institution established by God. This institution is under attack in America and throughout the world just as the institution of the brotherhood is; producing racism, and the institution of death; producing abortion and the destruction of human life within the mother's womb.

Institution is defined as *the act of initiating or establishing something.* As mentioned before, God established marriage between one man and one woman. The first being Adam and Eve. In Genesis Chapter 2, the story gives the account of Adam receiving another human being to be with him. God saw that Adam was alone (all one) and decided to make another human being like unto Adam, but somewhat different from Adam. This human would have the same God qualities just as Adam did but would have a different physical (biological) makeup than Adam. This human was called woman because she was taken out of the man and given a womb. She was given the name of Eve thus signifying that she would be the *mother* of all human beings. If you notice that man did not come out of a man, man was created by God and woman was made from created man. This makes it impossible for man to be compatible with another man or a woman to be compatible with another woman.

It amazes me that anyone can look in the Bible and find justification for a lifestyle other than what God established from the beginning of time. I mentioned earlier that the founding fathers took many of their ideas for the government from the Bible. At that time, the Bible was esteemed a very important part of life for those setting out to create an established order of government they knew would provide for a Godly life and lifestyle and secure the future for the generations to come. The attack on the constitution in the areas I previously spoke about is really an attack on the very Word of God. It wasn't the constitution that stated *"therefore shall a man leave his father and mother and cleave unto his wife and they shall be one flesh;" it was the Bible.* It wasn't the constitution that stated *"to have respect of persons is a sin;" it was the Bible.* It wasn't the constitution that stated that: *murder of any sort is a sin; it was the Bible.* It is very clear that the attack on the constitution is an actual attack on the Word of God.

I think that God knew what He was doing when he made a woman for Adam and not another man. For those women who are struggling with their sexual identity; let this serve as a viable example for you to understand that God did not make a mistake when He made you. Woman is
defined as "a man with a womb." So she is called a "Wombed Man." The womb is the place of conception and cultivation, designed by God to receive seed from the man and bear the harvest. Men do not have a womb. They are designed to provide the seed for the womb.

Any man or woman who questions whether he or she is a man or a woman can easily find out. You can find out by simply examining the parts of the body itself. Men do not have a womb; women do not have the seed. The man was physiologically designed with what he needed to produce life after his kind, as stated in Genesis 1:27. The woman was made with the necessary physical attributes to be able to receive the seed in her womb and have the seed cultivated until the time for the birth. She was also given breasts which provided milk for the nourishment of the new babe. As you can see, there's really no valid reason for there to be any gender confusion.

This subject of gender confusion has made its way all the way to the Supreme Court, and as recent history has proved, these ungodly men and women stand in agreement with those whose agendas are to destroy everything that God has established. God never deviates from His order. As a matter of fact, He is bound by the same order Himself. King David said that God's Word is forever settled in heaven (Ps. 119:89). God always watches over His Word to perform it. (Jeremiah 1: 12) and Isaiah said in chapter 55 that His Word will never return void of unfulfilled.

Agreement with God always produces positive results and disagreement with God will always produce negative results. It doesn't matter how you feel, or what someone else has said about an experience that they've had. Your life must be lived according to the pattern which God has established. The prophet Isaiah said "how can the thing created say to its creator 'why did you make me like this. (Isaiah 29:16) I can assure you that God only made the man Adam and the woman Eve.

God is defined as omniscient - knowing all things, and having *complete* knowledge and wisdom. He is the *only* omniscient one. The abortionist and those who choose to abort the life within them are placing themselves in the position of God Almighty when they take a life. They actually defy the creator of life by destroying life. So too do those who defy their own bodies saying to themselves, "There must have been a mistake made when I was born and therefore, I'm going to do something to change it." In Romans 1:17-32, there is an interesting account of the condition of the church that had been established by the Apostle Paul. This story really speaks to our present state as a Church. This church was like ours today - infected by the influence of the world. God never intended for the church to be influenced by the world. Jesus said that the church is the light of the world. (Matthew 5:14) If the light refuses to transform the darkness, the darkness begins to transform the light. This is why you see protestant denominations ordaining homosexual ministers and performing homosexual unions.

Racism, abortion and homosexuality are all a part of a particular culture designed by Satan to destroy God's creation.

Culture is defined as a *group of people who share beliefs and practices* or a *particular set of attitudes that characterizes the group of people.* The Church is a culture made up of believers in the Lord Jesus Christ. I do not know when, but at some point in history, a passive attitude concerning racism, abortion, and homosexuality and similar issues infiltrated the church, the consequences are being experienced all over the world. The true church culture is that of a violent group who share the belief that what their Lord has said is true; thus, pursuing that truth with reckless abandonment. As it says in Matthew 11:12, "the kingdom of heaven suffers violence and the violent take it by force." Violent is defined as marked by extreme force or sudden, intense activity; notably furious or vehement; extreme or intense; passionate; fervid; zealous. Those who had this particular attitude were able in just a few short years to turn the world upside down. Where is that culture of men and women who truly believe what God has said?

Here we read in Romans 1: 17-32:

For therein is the righteousness of God revealed from faith to faith: as it is written, the just shall live by faith. For the wrath of God is revealed from heaven against all ungodliness and unrighteousness of men, who hold the truth in unrighteousness; Because that which may be known of God is manifest in them; for God hath showed it unto them. For the invisible things of him from the creation of the world are clearly seen, being understood by the things that are made, even his eternal power and Godhead; so that they are without excuse: Because that, when they knew God, they glorified him not as God, neither were thankful; but became vain in their imaginations, and their foolish heart was darkened. Professing themselves to be wise, they became fools, and changed the glory of the incorruptible God into an image made like to corruptible man, and to birds, and four-footed beasts, and creeping things. Wherefore God also gave them up to uncleanness through the lusts of their own hearts, to dishonor their own bodies between themselves: Who changed the truth of God into a lie, and worshipped and served the creature more than the Creator, who is blessed forever. Amen. For this cause God gave them up unto vile affections: for even their women did change the natural use into that which is against nature: And likewise also the men, leaving the natural use of the woman, burned in their lust one toward another; men with men working that which is unseemly, and receiving in themselves that recompense of their error which was meet. And even as they did not like to retain God in their knowledge, God gave them over to a reprobate mind, to do those things which are not convenient.

It would be difficult for any believer to read this and not understand what God's intention for man is. To vote for any person who will stand in such bold contradiction and rebellion to God is in fact an act of bold contradiction and rebellion to God on their part. The Church must **WAKE UP** and **STAND UP** against such things as this.

The church will be held accountable and thereby, responsible for their actions during elections. In Luke 16, the Lord gives a parable concerning a steward who was accused of wasting his master's goods. The master calls for the steward and demands of him to give an account of his stewardship. In other words, he was saying "Have you been responsible with those things that I put into your trust and care?". This is a story that parallels what is happening in the church today. We have been afforded the privilege to participate in choosing those who will best represent the believer by being good stewards over the election ballot we place. What will we do with it, is it our right and privilege to choose? In the story of this steward, the goods belonged to the master. In the church's case, the votes (choice) belong to the Lord. What will we do with them? Will we vote (choose) for the Democrat or the Republican or the White or Black, the pro-choice or the pro-life, the liberal or the conservative, etc.?

In the book of Genesis chapters 13&19, the Bible speaks of Lot-Abram's nephew, who lived in the land of Sodom and Gomorrah. Sodom and Gomorrah was filled with all sorts of sexual perversion namely sodomy, which is homosexuality. This prompted the destruction of the entire population and ultimately the culture, including that of Lot and his family if they had not obeyed the messengers sent by God to get them out. It's really a sad story. It tells how a culture had become so inundated with the sin of homosexuality, that when God sent messengers to rescue Lot and his family, the men of the city attempted to engage in homosexual sex acts with them. When you take a historical look at Sodom and Gomorrah, you will discover that these cities did not initially begin with the citizens practicing the lifestyle they had come to know. Whenever the perversion began and was left unchecked, this counterculture began to evolve. I am certain that this is Satan's plan for America and other nations as well.

Please note that a famous part of this story is Lot's wife having been turned into a pillar of salt. (Genesis 19:26) What does this really mean, and more importantly, why did it happen? The Bible says that the angels gave Lot and his family explicit instructions to leave and not to look back. Some think that Lot's wife actually physically looked back to her home, to which I'm sure she had come to love. Did she actually turn her head and look back? I don't know but I do know what her problem was, is that she had grown accustomed to the culture and had probably become an ***apologetic participant seeking to be politically correct in the*** *culture*. Am I saying that she was engaging in homosexual acts? No I'm not, but Jesus said that 'If any person looks on another to lust after them, sin is committed *within their heart*.'(Matthew 5:27-28) This statement has been made and is very true: The Israelites were delivered from Egypt, but Egypt was still in them.

America and others have fallen prey to this same pattern, largely because the church has laid down to become the doormat to all sorts of sin and the gateway to all sorts of sinful ways. America the great melting pot, where what everybody believes has relevance regardless of what it is. As we talked about previously, the true church has a conqueror mentality. As a matter of fact, we are actually called "more than conquerors" (Romans 8:37). Remember, Jesus said 'Violent men press their way into the kingdom' (Matthew 11:12). There are those who are called environmentalists, and they are convinced that the ozone layer surrounding the earth's surface is eroding due to human negligence. They have set out to do whatever it takes to raise the awareness of the public to develop measures that can be taken to stop this. Global warming is a big issue and millions of dollars of taxpayer's money are being raised and spent to do research and put in the necessary legislation to prevent it.

Environmentalists are to be commended for their efforts to preserve our planet.

BUT, where's the church culture when it comes to racism - the destruction of brotherhood. Where's the church culture when it comes to abortions of all sorts and murder of the unborn? Where's the church culture when it comes to homosexuality and sexual union between two persons of the same sex?

In November 2003 the Massachusetts Supreme Judicial Court ruled that barring same-sex couples from civil marriage was unconstitutional. The Senate then asked the Court for an advisory opinion on the constitutionality of a proposed law that would bar same-sex couples from civil marriage but would create civil unions as a parallel institution, with all the same benefits, protections, rights and responsibilities under law. In February, the Court answered, "segregating same-sex unions from opposite-sex unions cannot possibly be held rationally to advance or preserve" the governmental aim of encouraging "stable adult relationships for the good of the individual and of the community, especially its children." Under this decision, the state of Massachusetts began issuing marriage licenses to same sex couples in May 2004.

This ruling is part of a larger public discussion of "marriage" and "family" that started in 1993 when the Hawaii Supreme Court ruled that laws denying same sex couples the right to marry violated state constitutional equal protection rights unless the state could show a "compelling reason" for such discrimination. In 1996, a trial court ruled that the state had no such compelling reason and the case headed back to the Supreme Court. Voters adopted a Constitutional amendment in 1998, before the final ruling was issued, giving the Legislature the power to reserve marriage to opposite-sex couples and effectively ending the lawsuit.

In April 2000, Vermont approved landmark legislation to recognize civil unions between same-sex couples, granting them virtually all the benefits, protections, and responsibilities that married couples have under Vermont law. The Vermont legislation was a result of the state Supreme Court ruling in *Baker* v. *Vermont* that said same-sex couples are entitled, under the state constitution's "Common Benefits Clause," to the same benefits and protections as married opposite-sex couples. The court ruled that the Vermont Legislature must decide how to provide these benefits and protections, either by legalizing marriage for same-sex couples or by establishing an alternative system. In April 2005, Connecticut became the first state to legalize civil unions without prompting from the courts.

The Vermont Legislature chose to preserve marriage as the "legally recognized union of one man and one woman," *but at the same time create a parallel system of civil unions for same-sex couples that go beyond existing "domestic partnership" and "reciprocal beneficiaries"* laws that exist in California and Hawaii and in many localities in the U.S. today. In October 2006, the New Jersey Supreme Court ordered the legislature to redefine marriage to include same-sex couples or establish a separate legal structure, such as civil unions, to give same-sex couples the same rights as heterosexual married couples. In late 2006, the New Jersey legislature passed a statute allowing civil unions beginning February 19, 2007. New Hampshire passed legislation authorizing civil unions which will take effect on January 1, 2008.

On May 15, 2008, the California Supreme

Court ruled that same-sex couples should have the right to marry. The ruling takes effect in mid-June but could be stayed by the courts for six months, which would allow California residents to vote on a proposed constitutional amendment defining marriage between a man and a woman. If the amendment passes in November, same-sex marriage would again be banned in California.

The present condition of America and others like it is due to the reality that the church has been too passive and thus too quiet. Not like the environmentalist who is pressing their way for change. This last reference concerning the state of California describes a ticking time bomb. Usually what becomes the political norm in states like California and New York will soon become the norm for the rest of the nation and then the world. California's decision to make it legal for two same-sex persons to obtain a marriage license could be the beginning of the new Sodom and Gomorrah culture.

It amazes me that within the local and state government of California that there was not and is not a Christian voice that was crying out, "Wait a minute!" Why was there no one outraged by this proposition? Where are those like the homosexual and pro-abortion groups who will fight to the death for what they believe? The mere fact that this legislation is on the books tells me that the church was somewhere in its passive posture not willing to get involved. As a result of the success of this legislation, there is a proposition for a homosexual curriculum to be taught in public schools in California. This type of curriculum and those like unto them are taught for the purpose of promoting the homosexual agenda and setting out to create a culture that will further strengthen a legislative hold of homosexuality on the people of America. In other words, if you teach your children that it's right and proper for a man and a woman to get married, then most likely your children will believe this and follow that example. On the other hand, if you teach or allow your child to be taught that it is right and proper to marry a person of the same gender as they are, they will usually follow the example given to them.

Here's where America is now: Since the first publication of How Would Jesus Vote, President

Barak Obama's push for Gay marriage, since taking office, President Obama and his administration has made historic strides to expand opportunities and advance equality and justice for all Americans, including Lesbian, Gay, Bisexual, Transgender, and Queer (LGBTQ) Americans. From major legislative achievements to historic court victories to important policy changes, the President has fought to promote the equal rights of all Americans — no matter who they are or who they love. That commitment to leveling the playing field and ensuring equal protection under the law is the bedrock principle this nation was founded on and has guided the President's actions in support of all Americans. And the progress the administration has made mirrors the changing views of the American people, who recognize that fairness and justice demand equality for all, including LGBTQ Americans. As I mentioned earlier that the LGBTQ agenda is an attack on the Word of God.

Here's a caption of the LGBTQ Manifest, there plan to make their lifestyle as normal, acceptable, promoted and protected by the government as they possibly can.

Our LGBT Manifesto

A manifesto for LGBT communities, developed by LGBT organisations

There is real opportunity for full equality of Lesbian, Gay, Bisexual & Trans people in the UK. We ask all political parties to embrace our community messages and sign up to our two main community asks.

Our Community Messages

Education
Educate all children & young people, at all levels, on gender & sexual diversity

Safety
Monitor & address homophobic, biphobic & transphobic hate crime

Wellbeing
Improve the mental, emotional & physical health of all LGBT people through increased awareness & improved practice

Access
Ensure LGBT people have equal access to public services

Our Asks of Political Parties

• Ensure all children & young people leave school with a thorough understanding of gender & sexual diversity through age-appropriate teaching at all levels, embedding learning within the curriculum & in particular SRE

• Improve the mental health of LGBT people through greater awareness raising of the issues faced, through better access to services & addressing homophobia, biphobia & transphobia within public services

This manifesto has been developed as a collaboration between LGBT organisations from across the UK. We invite you to engage with us to discuss our points and help make our asks a reality

Talk to us at LGBTmanifesto@lgbtconsortium.org.uk or on 0207 064 6500

Here's how they did under Obama's administration. The Obama Administration's record on social progress and equality includes:

- **Preventing Bullying and Hate Crimes against LGBT Americans** (the Matthew Shepard and James Byrd, Jr. Hate Crimes Prevention Act into law in October 2009)
- **Supporting LGBT Health** (In June 2009, President Obama issued a directive on same-sex domestic partner benefits, opening the door for the State Department to extend

the full range of legally available benefits and allowances to same-sex domestic partners of members of the Foreign Service sent to serve abroad.)

•   **Repealing Don't Ask, Don't Tell** (In February 2011, the President and Attorney General announced that the Department of Justice would no longer defend the Defense of Marriage Act's provision defining marriage as only between a man and woman, leading to the Supreme Court's landmark decisions holding the Act unconstitutional.)

•   **Protecting LGBT Americans against Discrimination** (In July 2014, the President signed an Executive Order prohibiting federal contractors from discriminating against any employee or applicant for employment "because of race, color, religion, sex, sexual orientation, gender identity, or national origin," continuing to set an example as a model employer that does right by its employees.)

•   **Taking Steps to Ensure LGBT Equality in Housing and Crime Prevention** (In January 2012 and in 2015, the President issued a final rule and subsequent guidance to ensure that the Department of Housing and Urban Development's core housing programs and services are open to all persons regardless of sexual orientation or gender identity.)

•   **Advancing and Protecting the Rights of LGBT Persons around the World** (The Obama administration continues to engage systematically with governments around the world to advance the rights of LGBT persons. The Administration's leadership has included various public statements and resolutions at the UN.)

•   **Recognizing LGBT History and Contributions** (On May 28, 2014, the Department of the Interior announced a new
National Park Service theme study to identify places and events associated with
the civil rights struggle of LGBT Americans and ensure that the agency is telling a complete story of America's heritage and history. (The results of the theme study are expected later this year.)

The LGBTQ manifesto is playing out right under our noses.

Anything that becomes culturally acceptable will eventually become culturally normal. When something becomes culturally normal society begins to adapt to it as in the case of cities of Sodom and Gomorrah.

How would Jesus Vote?

Chapter 6
POLITICAL PARTY

The church has to decide how it is going to conduct itself going forward, by asking two important questions. These are: 1. Do I pledge my allegiance to a political party? 2. Do I pledge my allegiance to my own conscience authority? I'm sure that many of you are asking what is meant by conscience authority. I will answer your question shortly, but first we need to discuss what political parties are and why they hold such dominance in the lives of those who attach themselves to them. Including Christians.

The definition for politics as we talked about in the beginning of this book is: *the theory and practice* of *government.* Notice *theory* and *practice* of *government.* Remember the definition for *theory* is defined as: *an idea* or *ideas formed by speculation.* What are ideas formed by speculation? *Speculation* is defined as: *reasoning based on **incomplete** information.* Now let's deal with the term *practice* of *government. Practice* is defined as: *the process* of *carrying out an idea, plan,* or *theory.* These definitions of the term politics really describe what many of our present-day politicians are doing. Shouldn't Christians be a part of the political process, since the process only consists of practicing ideas formed through speculation. The perfect person for leadership in every sphere of influence in America and throughout the world should be a Christian because the believer has complete information and need not speculate i.e. King Solomon. We know what's right and wrong based on the standards given to us in the Bible. How would Jesus vote?

Political parties are nearly as old as this nation

and they were established for the purpose of promoting a particular agenda. The proposed agenda would set out to establish something new or to oppose that which was previously established. The two dominant parties that we have today used to be one party called the Democratic - Republican Party. Due to some internal issues that could not be resolved, the Democratic - Republican Party split and became separate parties: The Democratic and Republican party. Although there are others today, these two are the most prominent of the parties.

When taking a very close look at any of the candidates running for the political office, those who are not dedicated believers will have things going on in their personal belief systems that we, as Christians, need to be concerned about, which could even lead you to decide to not vote for either of them. We also know that, for Christians not to be involved in the political process and not vote is just as bad as voting for the wrong person. So the reality is, someone has to get our vote.

Would Jesus vote for the democratic candidate or would He vote for the republican candidate? Would Jesus vote for the Black or the White candidate? Would Jesus vote for the Pro-life or the Pro-choice (death) candidate? Would Jesus vote for the candidates who support gay rights or for the one who supports the sanctity of marriage? These are questions as followers of Jesus we must answer. However, they cannot be answered using the politically correct way of doing things. *This answer is found within your own conscience authority.*

How would Jesus Vote?

Chapter 7
CONSCIENCE AUTHORITY

We've discussed three of the main issues that we face in America today and other nations as well, more importantly, a nation of believers. I raised those issues because you cannot deny that they do exist. Although there are some terrible things associated with them, these issues are very prevalent in every level of government. Within both the Democratic and Republican Parties there's a mess. Usually, things begin at the local level then moves to the state eventually ending at the federal level. We live within all three of these levels of government at one time and are affected for good or for bad depending on who's proposing what. Each of these issues are in some form or another being plastered within the consciousness of all those who give their attention to them. In other words, whatever you look at and listen to in a repetitious manner will begin to shape your perception and ultimately your beliefs.

The church has been and will be affected by the chaos that can be found in politics until we adhere to the way that God established for us to make right (righteous) choices. The church is presently divided just like the nation. There are pastors who are afraid to have politics as a topic of discussion in their churches for the fear of causing those in opposition with the others to get angry with him because of where he stands in the divide. *You talking about a mess.* If pastors and religious leaders do not educate their followers in the proper way to conduct themselves during an election. (The political process) How are they supposed to know? *After all the pastor is the shepherd whose responsibility is the lead the sheep.*

For a pastor to abdicate his responsibility to involve his flock in the political process is reprehensible and irresponsible. Making the sheep meat for the enemy. Jeremiah said that God would raise up pastors after His heart that would feed (educate) the sheep not fleece the sheep by not informing them of the dangers of not voting responsibly. As a result of this the church has been left to the media to educate them or should I say indoctrinate them? The media is doing it's very best to indoctrinate them and they are succeeding. Is It no wonder that we're divided by political party affiliation, we are divided by race, gender and we are divided by what is morally right. Those of us who have been in the church for any length of time have no doubt heard this statement, "As the head goes so does the body". King Solomon said that *when the righteous are in authority the people rejoice but when the wicked bear rule the people mourn* (Proverbs 29:2). It amazes me as to how much the church resembles the world. There's only one race of people it's the human race, there's only one way to vote (choose) for any candidate and that's the way that God would have you vote (choose). No one chose their race or gender neither can we as Christians choose who we vote for based on information gathered solely from *outside sources*. I know that that is a bold statement but keep reading and you'll come to agree with the statement. Jesus was responsible for developing his followers in conscience authority.

The church must be reminded that there is only **one voice** and **with that voice, God speaks to _all_ of his children (not black, white, democrat, republican, male or female, conservative or liberal) the same thing**. If God is saying just one thing to the believer but the believer has been polarized to think a certain way because of the indoctrination of the media and others, it is highly possible that the believer will hear another voice. This is why the diehard allegiance to a party for a believer is extremely dangerous. Because it places you at the disadvantage of having to decipher between multiple voices.

When the church is **Democrat or Republican** *this is called DIVISION*. Jesus said in Mt. 12 "if any house, city or kingdom is divided against itself it cannot stand but SHALL come to desolation. Division means more than one, please remember that there's only one body of Christ not many-body of Christ. The apostle Paul ask the Corinthian church 'was Christ divided?'. You see when we choose to align ourselves with a party because of a tradition we run the risk of being deceived by the other voice. *I am convinced that if the church were to take an independent nonpartisan position that the church could begin to influence politics and our culture.*

But make no mistake about it that there are many in the church that feel that the voice of their party is more important than the voice of the shepherd who will never lead then astray. Conscience authority is of the utmost importance for the believer to understand. I pray that the church will wake up from its divisive nightmare.

Conscience is defined as The internal sense of what is right and wrong that governs one's thoughts and actions, urging him or her to do right rather than wrong. Authority is defined as: Law source of precedent or principle: a law or legal decision that is cited as establishing a precedent or a principle.

To sum it all up, the Lord Jesus said that the

Holy Spirit would lead and guide the believer into **all truth**; even **voting truth**. (John 16:13) The truth that is revealed to the believer by the Holy Spirit establishes in him or her a sense of knowing what's right and wrong. The truth that is revealed to the believer is an already established precedent and or principle. Jesus said, "…that you will know the truth and the truth will make you free" (John 8:32). Psalms 119 speaks explicitly concerning the word of God as the law of God. David said "I have hid your word in my heart that I might not sin against you. (Psalms 119:11)

The voting position of the believer is that of conscience authority. The Holy Spirit is the authority of the conscience. The conscience is the part of the human mind that is aware of the feelings, thoughts, and surroundings. Therefore, the Holy Spirit is the authority of all life, whether the person who has life acknowledges Him or not. It doesn't matter, He is the authority. *When conscience authority rules,* all opposing arguments have to come to an end. All battles are fought and victories won in the conscious part of the mind. There's only one winner in this game of life and it's the one who plays the game according to the rules written by the author and the creator of the game-the Almighty God.

The Lord Jesus was established in conscience authority. The writer of the book of Hebrews says of Jesus that though He were a son yet He *learned* obedience by the thing which He suffered (Hebrew 5:8). Notice that His obedience was learned. The believer has been the student of the world and not the Holy Spirit. If the believer remains content to be the world's student, they will eventually graduate to the failure of their nation. Jesus had to learn obedience.

Who was His teacher? Were they the scribes and Pharisees or the religious leaders of his day? Was it the Roman Government? Or maybe it was those who were sinners around him. If Jesus had been influenced by any of these, He would have never completed His assignment. However, we know that He did complete it.

Not only did He complete it, but He succeeded against all odds; such as becoming the human sacrifice that God required for the sins of the whole entire world. When He was pressed out of human measure in the garden of Gethsemane, where His sweat was as drops of blood, He used every bit of human reasoning to convince Himself and His Father that there had to be another way to rectify the sin issue. Subsequently, because of His *conscience authority,* He was compelled to utter these words, "Not my will (Father), but yours be done." He understood that He was not here for His own benefit but for the benefit of those who needed His obedience.

He had learned to honor God in all that He did. John 5:19-20 says, Jesus said to those who opposed him "The Son can do nothing of himself, but what he sees the father do. This is what the Son does likewise." The next verse must find its way into your heart. It is crucial that you hear this. "***The father loves the Son and <u>shows him all things that he is doing and he will show greater works than these</u> so that you may marvel***." How was he established in conscience authority? He spoke to his followers in Matthew 11 saying, "Come unto me all who are burdened and heavy laden. Take my yoke upon you and learn of me." He speaks of this yoke that He had taken possession of. And He offered his yoke to all those who needed rest. This yoke had to be something special if it could do what He alleged it would. In Hebrews 5:8 it says that Jesus "learned obedience by the things that He suffered." In order to learn most anything, you must have an instructor who is someone who knows what you don't know, but has a desire for you to know what they know.

What Jesus had learned provided the yoke He now possessed. This yoke was His conscience authority. Conscience authority (yoke) is developed as we learn of Him. During any political process, it is the job of the candidates to educate the masses on his or her desire to represent them. This is done by making promises to do certain things for them and change things that need to be changed for their benefit. They will also attempt to educate you on their opponents by bringing their negative past to the forefront for everyone to see.

The media is obliged to flood the airways with the "instructor's" messages. Jesus' instructor was His Father, and as a result of Jesus' being a good student (disciple), He was able to develop the yoke that would help Him through the most difficult times in His life. It was this yoke of conscience authority that caused him to go through the betrayal and denial of His close friends and the hate-filled suffering that He endured from His own family, race and the Romans who killed Him. It was this yoke that caused Him to humble Himself and be blindfolded and hit in the face, spit in the face, have His beard plucked out, and taken to a whipping post established for criminals and to beating repeatedly until His bowels were exposed. It was this yoke that caused Him to lay still and allow the nails to be driven into His hands and feet. This is the same yoke that He offered everyone who needed peace of mind and rest. ***His yoke com-***

pelled Him and propelled Him to safely trust what
He had learned.

Just like the ox that is plowing the field the controlling factor for the ox is the yoke around his neck. This yoke gave the person in control of the ox the ability to direct the movement of the ox. Without this yoke, the ox would have free reign and because of its nature it could have done some tremendous damage to the field that He was working in and to the person or persons present. Without Jesus' yoke He might have failed in following the direction of the Holy Spirit who was leading Him in doing only those things that pleased His Father. We can no longer allow tradition and media to be our teacher. We can see that whatever information we receive from tradition and the media will be developed in us, thus becoming our conscience authority. (yoke)

We are commanded to "come out from among them and be ye separate." (2 Corinthians 6:17) This is not a contradiction of what I said earlier. We need a strong voice in every area in our society, but that voice has to speak what it hears the Father say. Jesus was able to do this because His conscience was established in righteousness. Conscience - the internal sense of what is right and wrong that governs someone's thoughts and actions, urging him or her to do right rather than wrong. This can clearly be seen in the Lord Jesus.

When the believer is positioned under the rule of conscience authority, this authority rejects political correctness, and steers the believer in the morally right direction. The problem with the believer in the voting process is not a problem with politics, but the solution of needing a **moral fix**.

This moral fix is of the utmost importance for America and the world. A moral fix is the only direction in which America and other nations can proceed in in order to turn what appears to be a Titanic-like scenario around. The *Titanic,* whose improbable demise came, in spite of the fact that it had used some of the most advanced technology available at that time. It was, before the sinking, popularly believed to be "unsinkable". It was a great shock to many-that despite the advanced technology and experienced crew-the *Titanic* sank, with a great loss of life.

America is known throughout the world as a superpower, and not just a world power. Much like the Titanic which was a world power among passenger ships, America has been blessed by God to have some of the greatest technology in the world as well as some of the world's most influential people *making* it the best ship on the sea. Just like the Titanic, America has taken the foundational principles that it was built upon for granted. If it maintains its present course, it will certainly do what many think is improbable-crash and the loss of life will be great. America is in desperate need of a moral fix and I can assure you that it will not occur in the political mix. The political mix is nothing but a huge political mess that has caused all of America and much of the world to be affected negatively by it. Unless the believer finds his way within this mix, it will remain a mess.

How Would Jesus Vote?

Chapter 8
POLITICAL CORRECTNESS
OR
MORAL RIGHTNESS

Should the believer be concerned about being politically correct or should he or she be concerned about being morally right? There are many stories in the Bible that give answers to these questions for us. The one that I want to talk about is found in the New Testament. In the books of Matthew and John is the story of a king named Herod. He was king during the time of John the Baptist and the Lord Jesus Christ. History reveals that Herod had gotten married to the daughter of the King of Arabia but later he repudiated her after which he married his brother's wife whose name was Herodias.

John the Baptist knew of this union. I'm sure it had become public knowledge. However, John the Baptist did not just sit back passively on his hands and not deal with it. John did what the church should have done when Mrs. O'Hara sought to remove prayer out of the public schools and when a fornicating mother of two, who was pregnant with her third child, decided that she did not want the burden of having a third distraction to deal with and when the present-day homosexual community is making it a pressing agenda to make it legislatively right to LEGALLY marry someone of the same sex. These agendas and those like them are somehow convinced that if the government approves the agenda, this makes it right and no one else has the *right* to say anything about it.

John did not allow the position of the person who was in the wrong to intimidate him. He was interested in the *things* that were done that contradicted the established order of God. John confronted the issue with confident, violent aggression. It wasn't time to be *politically correct.* It was time to be *morally right.*

The term of political correctness is not that old nonetheless it is spreading its way like a wildfire through the Christian nations. Take a look at this summary. *Variations of this speech have been delivered to various AIA conferences including the 2000 Conservative University at American University.*

Where does all this stuff that you've heard about this morning - the victim feminism, the gay rights movement, the invented statistics, the rewritten history, the lies, the demands, all the rest of it - where does it come from? For the first time in our history,

Americans have to be fearful of *what they say, of what they write, and of what they think. They have to be afraid of using the wrong word, a word denounced as offensive or insensitive, or racist, sexist, or homophobic.*

We have seen other countries, particularly in this century, where this has been the case. And we have always regarded them with a mixture of pity, and to be truthful, some amusement, because it has struck us as so strange that people would allow a situation to develop where they would be afraid of what words they used. But we now have this situation in this country. We have it primarily on college campuses, but it is spreading throughout the whole society. Where does it come from? What is it? We call it "Political Correctness." The name originated as something of a joke, literally in a comic strip, and we tend still to think of it as only half-serious. In fact, it's deadly serious. It is the great disease of our century, the disease that has left tens of millions of people dead in Europe, in Russia, in China, indeed around the world. It is the disease of ideology. PC is not funny. PC is deadly serious.

The totalitarian nature of Political Correctness is revealed nowhere more clearly than on college campuses where the student or faculty member who dares to cross any of the lines set up by the gender feminist or the homosexual-rights activists, or the local black or Hispanic group, or any of the other sainted "victims" groups that PC revolves around, quickly find themselves in judicial trouble. Within the small legal system of the college, they face formal charges - some star- chamber proceeding - and punishment. That is a little look into the future that Political Correctness intends for the nation as a whole.

If John the Baptist was here today, he would be appalled at the way things are. His disgust and displeasure would no doubt cause a righteous indignation to rise up in him. This righteous indignation would cause him to confront the sin issue. The church's passivity doesn't look anything like that of John's ambition. John was on an assignment to see when something was out of place and do what was right and proper to fix it. In the case with King Herod, his present marriage was against the established order of God. John could have taken the position of one saying "it's not any of my business" or a "who cares" mentality. But because John was on an **assignment**, (Mt. 28:18-20) he was compelled to speak against the adulterous situation.

Political correctness has had and is having a dulling effect on the word of God. Hebrews 4, says for the word of God is quick, and powerful, and sharper than any two-edged sword, piercing even to the dividing asunder of soul and spirit, and of the joints and marrow, and is a discerner of the thoughts and intents of the heart. This is the same word that David said he had hidden it in his heart that he might not sin against God. It's the same word that Isaiah said that would not return unto God void and it's the same word the Lord used in creating everything that is in Genesis chapter one. It's the same word that help establish this once great nation.

Even the church is forced to be politically correct today. There is a threat to censor those church leaders who will use words such as homosexuals and others like them. This impending threat has taken the edge off of word of God and thereby minimized its ability to cause conviction in those who are either practicing the lifestyle and content to deem it as acceptable. The Apostle Paul said in Romans that how can the people hear without a preacher, he also said that God would use the foolishness of preaching to cause men to be saved. There is life-changing power in the word just as it is, it has the ability to cut through theory and conjecture and even speculation but, when it is minimized by the efforts of men, it loses its power to cut away at whatever circumstance the hearer is involved in at the time. The church cannot be guilty any longer of being a willing participant

in the destructive activity of being politically correct.

How Would Jesus Vote?

Chapter 9
Separation of Church and State

I pledge allegiance to the Flag of The United States of America, and to the Republic for which it stands: *(one Nation) (under God) **(indivisible),*** With Liberty and Justice for all.

In the last chapter, we talked about John the Baptist and his refusal to be politically correct but remain morally right under some very extreme circumstances. John was actually confronting the King of Israel, which just did not seem like something a man of John's status would attempt to do. After all, Herod was the king and the king usually controls everything, including the lives of those whom he governs.

A circumspect look into this story of John the Baptist and King Herod reveals that there are two types of governments represented. The first and not necessarily in the order of importance is the state. The second is the church. Someone in America decided many years ago that these needed to be separate. I'm going to make an effort to explain to you why this cannot and why it has not worked. As a matter of fact, many of the problems that are present within our nation and others are due largely to this separation.

Here are some examples: no more prayer in the public schools, removal of the Ten Commandments from federal courtrooms and other public places and recently the move of an atheist group to remove "In God We Trust" off of America's money. Although the standard of church and state separation was established but not constitutional, it is clearly seen that there were areas where the church and the state were in partnership.

This partnership between the two played a vital role in America becoming a great nation. I would love to say "the greatest nation", but I don't think we hold that status any longer. The decline in our nation is a direct result of the decline in the presence of morality. This decline in morality is a result of the separation of the church in America and the government. Whenever a Christian culture decides to vote against Christ's established order that which was once a Christian culture now becomes a culture of all sorts of unrighteousness.

In 1 Samuel, we read that the children of Israel had been governed by God through the prophets and the priests of that day. These men were responsible for the proper legislation of that which was right and proper. Before there was the state of Israel, there was the Church-which simply represents God. The Church represents the spiritual "where and who" God is, and the State represents the natural "where and who" man is.

This system was working very well as far as God was concerned. However, the children of Israel had begun to be influenced by the other nations around them (the media) who had men that they could look upon and receive instruction from. The Israelites had been warned by God not to involve themselves with the nations around them. God knew that they would be influenced by those around them rather than be the influencing agent they were designed to be. Their desire for a king came from outside influence.

America has been called the great melting pot because it has welcomed nearly any and everyone who has displayed the desire to come here. As a result of this many of the religious ideals of those who have come to America have made their way into our society and the consequences have been devastating to our Christian culture. Our universities have become a giant stage and platform for many of these religious ideals causing utter confusion among unsuspecting students-many of which came from Christian homes. They leave home a devout believer and return home after a semester confused about what they believe. As a result, this has begun the proliferation of evil in every arena of life.

In Israel, the culture had been established for quite some time. Whenever there arose those who opposed the established order, they were immediately dealt with in a way God chose. The swift dealing with the problem (judgment) sent the message that God hasn't changed His mind about His established order. The order is the same and must be adhered to at any cost. This is why John the Baptist, who represented the Church was so adamant about confronting the king Herod, who represented the ungodly state.

Samuel was the priest and prophet for Israel. He was the liaison between God and Israel. Israel's overwhelming desire to have a puppet king was granted by God even though He counseled them against the idea. Saul was chosen to be the king by God but it was Samuel who had to convey what it was that God intended. Samuel was the spokesman for God in the earth.

This would create a model that resembles the church and state. Remember, the Church represents the spiritual (heaven) and the State represents the natural (earth). From this time on, you will find throughout Israel's history the church and state connection and partnership; not church and state separation. Subsequently, whenever there was a separation in the church and state, there were always problems. The problems would always be resolved when the church and state returned to their partnership.

The state was not designed to exist alone and be independent. Without the church, the state has to fail because the state is designed to only resemble the church. The Lord Jesus put it this way as He responded to a request of His disciples to teach them how to pray. "When you pray, say "our Father who is in heaven; holy is your name. Your Kingdom come. Your will be done on EARTH as it is in HEAVEN."(Matthew 6:8-13) Please notice that Heaven is the place where all creation originated. Jesus knew the order established by God and was bound to adhere to that order. Jesus said in essence, that the earth is to look like heaven but man's participation is necessary.

If Earth is to look like heaven, there has to be an agent of conversion in the Earth to ensure this. When you look at John the Baptist's dealings with King Herod, you can see that John's position was to make sure that what had been established as right and proper was adhered to. Please get this:

Earth is designed by God to look like Heaven. John knew that there was no adultery in heaven and he understood that if he didn't confront this violation, this could very well become the precedent that all men would begin to govern their lives by.

This clearly paints the picture of what we see throughout America and other nations today: Same-sex unions, racism, the murder of the unborn, no prayer for Christians in school, In God We Trust took off of our money, Globalism, One World Government, etc. These and others like them were ideals that someone had and was passionate enough about them, so much so that they would do anything possible to get their ideals into the mainstream of society.

Where's John the Baptist (Church) when you (State) needs him. The State needs the Church. The king needs the priest and prophet. Most importantly is that the church is the source of the state and whenever you separate anything from its source the thing will die. The state without the church in America is doom for destruction.

How Would Jesus Vote?

Chapter 10
PRIEST-PROPHET AND KING CORROBORATION

Again the king represents the state (natural). The priest/prophet represents the church (spiritual). After the Kingdom had been established in Israel, this governmental model would be used as the stage and established platform that Israel was to live by. When you look at Israel, you can see this connection between the priest/prophet and the king. There was a corroboration between the two called a partnership. This partnership was not set up by man, but rather by God. As pointed out earlier, God's desire and design for man is that the earth would resemble heaven. Mt. 6:10

The order went something like this: when decisions needed to be made by the king concerning his kingdom, he would consult the priest or the prophet, the priest/ prophet would inform the king concerning the direction to proceed in for the kingdom. The priest/prophet would pray and seek the face of God, (the creator of the kingdom). The priest/prophet would be given explicit instructions as to what to do. The priest/prophet would return from the presence of God and convey those instructions that came from

God to the king. The king would adhere to the instruction given to him by the priest/prophet. In all of the cases found throughout the Bible where this was the order, there would always, without fail, be a positive outcome.

In the book of ISamuel12:14-15, after Saul had become king, he was given some specific instructions concerning the kingdom. Samuel also gave the children of Israel some vital instructions that would cause them to succeed throughout their existence.

If ye will fear the LORD, and serve him, and obey his voice, and not rebel against the commandment of the LORD, then shall both ye and also the king that reigneth over you continue following the LORD your God: But if ye will not obey the voice of the LORD, but rebel against the commandment of the LORD, then shall the hand of the LORD be against you, as it was against your fathers.

King Saul found that what God had commanded through Samuel was true.

And he tarried seven days, according to the set time that Samuel had appointed: but Samuel came not to Gilgal; and the people were scattered from him. And Saul said, Bring hither a burnt offering to me, and peace offerings. And he offered the burnt offering. And it came to pass, that as soon as he had made an end of offering the burnt offering, behold, Samuel came; and Saul went out to meet him, that he might salute him. And Samuel said, What hast thou done? And Saul said, Because I saw that the people were scattered from me, and that thou camest not within the days appointed, and that the Philistines gathered themselves together at Michmash; Therefore said I, The Philistines will come down now upon me to Gilgal, and I have not made supplication unto the LORD: I forced myself therefore, and offered a burnt offering,. And Samuel said to Saul, Thou hast done foolishly: thou hast not kept the commandment of the LORD thy God, which he commanded thee: for now would the LORD have established thy kingdom upon Israel for ever. But now thy kingdom shall not continue: the LORD hath sought him a man after his own heart, and the LORD hath commanded him to be captain over his people, because thou hast not kept that which the LORD commanded thee. (1 Samuel 12:8-14)

Saul (King) who represented the State violated the order sent by God and established by Samuel (Priest/Prophet) who represented the Church. God never intended for any king to govern separate from his influence. Any attempt to do so would certainly yield such results as we see written in the above scriptures. God never intended for the church to operate outside of His Sovereign Providence. Providence is defined as: foresight or forethought. God knows all and He sees all. Any nation who decides to alienate God, who is the architect, has and will continue to yield what we are seeing in our society today. God promised that if King Saul would govern according to His established order, he would always succeed.

There must be partnership between the Priest/ Prophet and the King. (Church and State) There must be an agreement between the Priest/Prophet and the King (Church and State). This connection between the Priest/Prophet and King paramount in order for the kingdom to succeed. Without these, failure is certain. This can be clearly seen throughout Israel's history. God will never relinquish ultimate control over His creation. He said in Psalms 24:1 that "the earth is the Lord's and fullness thereof', but He must have willing and informed vessels that will yield themselves to Him for His purposes to be established in the Earth. The world needs the unified church like never before. Only the church has the proper connection with God. God has all the necessary information needed for all nations including America.

Canaan was the land that God had promised to Abraham. Canaan would be a very prosperous land with everything the Israelites would need and desire. God called it a land flowing with milk and honey. Some in the world today and in the past, say that America resembles this land of Canaan.

America has been labeled "the land of opportunity and land of promise". In the previous paragraph, we discussed a little history on the origination and the establishment of a government with Saul being the first King. Eventually the land became separated into two parts. You had Canaan, the Promised Land and then Israel and Judah within the promise land.

This resembles the American political structure. One land with two political systems vying for control of the whole. In Canaan, among the two entities each of these had a leader. The leader was responsible for the proper legislation of God's ideals. Notice that I said *God's* Ideals. There had to be concert between the two, which was of the utmost importance if they were to remain in right standing with God and thereby reap the benefits of being in that land which had been promised by God. Within the long list of leaders for both Judah and Israel, there is a great despairing difference between those who were in agreement with, in partnership with, and connected to God and those who weren't.

A great man of God by the name of Dr. Morris Cerullo whom I admire made the statement that all truth is parallel. What a parallel we're seeing here. Let's remember that God established how the government was to operate under Samuel and King Saul's leadership. As long as they adhered to what had been established by God, they prospered and succeeded. Saul's eventual rebellion lost him his leadership position. Soon afterward, David, who God called a man after His own heart, began to reign. The whole of Canaan was under David and after David's death his son Solomon's rule.

When Solomon died things began to change and became progressively worse. The split and separation of the kingdom was not just a split in the governmental system but it is a disconnect from the source (God). This split created division throughout Canaan and would eventually be the demise of the kingdom. Wherever there is division there are multiple visions. God established the Kingdom according to His plan and purposes (His vision) when the kingdom split more visions surfaced. Finally, there were three visions where there was originally one. As a result of this many terrible things begin to happen in Canaan. Judah was captured by Babylon and Israel was captured by Assyria. Both losing the very land of promise, the land of freedom and the land of opportunity.

America is beginning to resemble the old Canaan. The once coveted land that had been blessed by God. God is only one God and He has only one voice that he speaks with. The church has fallen into a divisive position. Some in the church are Democrat and some are Republican as I said earlier. I thought we were all one body hearing the same voice that speaks to the entire body of Christ the same words.

The church in any nation must hear the one and same voice that speaks to all of his children the same thing and take a bold stand for righteousness, right now. If we are going to continue to enjoy the freedom that we have been afforded and come to love, we must stand for righteousness. ***We are going to have to make the voice of the Lord resound throughout every courthouse, classroom, abortion clinic, shopping mall, movie set, boardroom and the white house itself.***

We must start by going to the pulpits, and then to the podiums of every courthouse, every schoolhouse and boardroom that are in opposition to the order of God and then to the polls. No longer can we stand idly by and allow this kingdom to be divided and like Canaan eventually taken from us. If heaven has little or no influence in the manner by which a nation is governed, then

I suggest that we no longer consider ourselves as a part of the church, but rather a willing participant among those who are trying to destroy everything that God is in America.

We must answer this question. As a Christian you have been given the unique privilege to be able to communicate with God. This communication comes because of our connection to Him. We are in covenant relationship with Him; a covenant that has been established by the very shed blood of His Son. As long as we are covered by the blood we remain connected to Him. This connection places us in partnership with Him. Jesus was in constant communication with the Father which is why He stated in John 5 that "I only do what I see my Father do" and in another place He said I only say what my father says. This is why He could be successful in all of His endeavors. He sought to please God with all of His heart, soul, and mind.

He would go into desert places alone just to commune with His Father. It was through Jesus' untiring efforts to please His Father that He developed the ability to hear and recognize His Father's voice. Jesus said of his followers in John 10:4-5,27 that "My sheep know my voice and a stranger they will not follow."

To be a Christian means to be Christ-like. Which means to be like Christ. How was Christ? Christ was always going about doing His Fathers business. He knew the voice of God. Not only did He know the voice of God, He knew that knowing the voice of God was His lifeline. Jesus drew the parable for His followers from the shepherds of His day who had been in such communication with their sheep, that eventually they knew His voice and only His voice.

The stranger's voice is the counterfeit voice. It sounds similar but it's not the same. The church has listened to a counterfeit voice in the past as it relates to politics. Why did we listen to that Counterfeit voice? The answer is simple. It is because the world's voice sounds like God's voice. As in the case of the sheep who follow the stranger, they followed him right into their own destruction. So too have many Christians fallen prey in the same manner.

There are many voices resounding throughout the land during the times to elect new leadership, for example, the Democratic and the Republican voices. How do you hear God's voice among these very loud voices? We are told that God's voice is sometimes like a still small voice. Remember Jesus had to steal away to get away from the many voices surrounding Him so that He could be sure that He heard the right voice.

I want to challenge those of you who have made it this far in this timely journey to be like Jesus concerning the political process. Each election going forward will prove to be crucial for the survival and continued blessing of our nation and the world as we have known and come to love. If the church misses it in any election in the future, I believe that the church will enter into a period of suffering as we in America have never known before. Listen to what Peter said in his first book written to churches that were in five different cities.

For the time is come that judgment must begin at the house of God: and if it first begin at us, what shall the end be of them that obey not the gospel of God? And if the righteous scarcely be saved, where shall the ungodly and the sinner appear? Wherefore let them that suffer according to the will of God commit the keeping of their souls to him in well doing, as unto a faithful Creator. (1 Peter 4:17-19)

The Church is the light and salt in the world. Light is for illumination and salt is for seasoning and preservation. If the Church is in judgment, the survival of our nation has to be in question. America will soon become a byword. America, the once-great superpower will be the word on the street around the world.

Satan has attempted to destroy America from the outside to no avail. So he has turned his focus to the inside. He is using people within this nation as instruments for the purpose of destroying this nation, whose anthem is "God Bless America."

We have talked about the political process in America. The church goes through this Democrat and Republican process as well. This bothers me because if God has one voice and the Bible is clear that He does, how can Christians who say they know the voice of God bind themselves to one political party, while others who also profess to be Christian say they know the voice of God and bind themselves to the other party. However, they both say they hear God in the matter. *God is not schizophrenic and he certainly can't be double-minded.*

James 1:8 says that a "double-minded man is

unstable in all his ways" and because he's doubled minded, he would not receive anything from the Lord. All Christians are from one source. Paul posed the question to the Corinthian church, "Is Christ divided?" (1 Cor. 1:13). No, He is not divided but when you look at the church, you can clearly see that there is much division within the church. America is divided by political parties and by race and unfortunately, the church is divided much the same way as well.

When the church recognizes that there is a problem, it must be willing to deal with it. During my research, I have talked to church leaders from around the country. Many of them spoke of the issues that we talked about earlier in the book and others spoke concerning their party's preference. I have heard very few speak of the things that you and I have talked about up to this point. It's as if they're unaware of the process that every successful person throughout the Bible went through to be a success. *They all heard the voice of God and followed it.*

Another bigger mess in the church as it relates to the political process is the issue of the black vote and the white vote. Traditionally, black Christians of all religious and social backgrounds vote for the Democratic candidates and most white middle to upper-class Protestants and Catholics vote for the Republican candidates.

The responsibility of every Christian is not to be caught up in the divisiveness of the political process, but to be caught up as Moses was when he went up on Mount Sinai to commune with God. The Bible says while he was there he got caught up in the glory of God and stayed there for forty days and forty nights. (Exodus 24:18) He heard God's voice and when he came down from the mountain, he was able to legislate what God had given him for his people. Are you sure you're hearing God's voice?

I spoke earlier about how pastors in the past abdicated their responsibility to preach against racism from their pulpits and how that the withholding (censoring) the truth concerning racism has had an adverse effect on society. It is true that what the church does should affect our society (state) but in a way that causes reconciliation, not alienation. Shouldn't the state be following the church? I'm certain that it should be.

I'm going to shift to our current day pastors and church leaders as it relates to the RESPONSI-BILITY to equip its followers in the political process. Shouldn't the members of the body of Christ, the Church, follow the head of the church, Christ? The apostle Paul said to Follow me as I follow Christ. Some pastors and church leaders have done a decent job equipping its followers in some areas such as salvation, prosperity, etc. But very few have equipped its followers in the political process. I'm sure that there may be several reasons for this so I won't speculate. It amazes me that most pastors and church leaders fail to realize that those they are leading are a part of the state. What I mean by this is that most, if not all of the congregation, work, shop, and go to school in a secular environment and unfortunately spend the majority of their time in similar environments. Statistics prove that the average Christian only attend church services once a week, which leaves the balance of their time as I said in a secular environment.

I was in a meeting with a pastor of a

30,000-member church and the subject of politics came up and the pastor said emphatically that he doesn't discuss politics in his church BECAUSE IT MIGHT DIVIDE THE CHURCH. Here's the reality, his church is already divided because he won't discuss politics. Again this book is not written to try and convince you or anyone, who you should vote for in any election but rather convince you that if you are a leader, you have the responsibility to prepare those who follow you to be equipped in the political process.

King Solomon said in Proverbs chapter 3:5-6, Trust in the Lord with all thine heart; and lean not unto thine own understanding. In all thy ways acknowledge him, and he shall direct thy paths. Somehow, some pastors and church leaders have forgotten this passage and others like it. In "ALL YOUR WAYS" includes "POLITICS'.

If "all your ways" include politics, where does the church member go to get equipped *in the ways* of politics if not from the church. Some of you may argue that they can get that information from their traditions, from the media and or the indoctrination centers that the public schools and universities have become. We have already highlighted the detriment of those educational resources.

The local church must become more than a religious center and local pastors have to become-more than religious leaders. Pastors must make the local church become the cultural center of society. The church represents the kingdom and King David said in Ps. 103:19 that God's kingdom rules over all kingdoms. Isn't it wonderful that Jesus said that you (the church) are the light of the world and the salt of the earth. Two of the most powerfully influential substances in the world designed to affect everything that they encounter.

How would Jesus Vote?

Chapter 11
TO VOTE YOUR CONSCIENCE IS TO VOTE GOD'S HEART

Among the candidates regardless of their race, gender or political affiliation, only God knows who the right person is for the job. *The only way to use your vote wisely is to know what God knows.* **The only way to do this is to know God's voice. He will tell you who to vote for**. I emphasis the importance of this again. The church hears the one voice. The apostle Paul said that we are to think the same thing. You can't do that unless you hear the same thing. It was God who told Samuel who the first King of Israel should be. It was God who told Samuel that Saul had failed in his responsibility as king and that he would be replaced by someone who had a heart after God's heart. It was God who told Samuel who that person was David, the man after God's own heart. This means he was a man who, like Jesus and Moses would seek to know God's voice for the purpose of carrying out His will in the earth and in his case, Israel.

Samuel was a priest and a prophet. He was responsible for hearing God's voice concerning the kingdom and then conveying the information to the king; at which time the king would set out to legislate what it was that God had said. The time had come for another king to sit on the throne because the present king Saul had rejected God's instructions. God told Samuel to go to a certain city to a certain man's house and anoint one of his sons to be the next king. Please notice how detailed the instructions were. As believers, we can know the voice of God without fail. If we follow that voice it will always lead us to a victorious outcome.

Samuel was sent to Jesse's house with instructions to anoint the next king of Israel. Although Samuel knew the voice of God, he was about to make the mistake that many believers have and will make because they fail to follow proper instructions because of familiarity and logic. Let's pick up the story in ISamuel16: 6-13.

And it came to pass, when they were come, that he looked on Eliab, and said, Surely the Lord's anointed is before him But the LORD said unto Samuel, Look not on his countenance, or on the height of his stature; because I have refused him: for the LORD seeth not as man seeth; for man looketh on the outward appearance but the LORD looketh on the heart. Then Jesse called Abinadab, and made him pass before Samuel. And he said, Neither hath the LORD chosen this. Then Jesse made Shammah to pass by. And he said, Neither hath the LORD chosen this. Again, Jesse made seven of his sons to pass before Samuel. And Samuel said unto Jesse, The LORD hath not chosen these. And Samuel said unto Jesse, Are here all thy children? And he said, There remaineth yet the youngest, and, behold, he keepeth the sheep. And Samuel said unto Jesse, Send and fetch him: for we will not sit down till he come hither. And he sent, and brought him in. Now he was ruddy, and withal of a beautiful countenance, and goodly to look to. And the LORD said, Arise, anoint him: for this is he. Then Samuel took the horn of oil, and anointed him in the midst of his brethren: and the spirit of the LORD came upon David from that day forward So Samuel rose up, and went to Ramah.

Samuel was about to fail in his assignment because he was, like so many believers today, looking on the outside and making choices. This is why racism is still alive and well in the Church. Eliab probably reminded Samuel of Saul. The Bible says that Saul stood head and shoulders above everyone else. Even Samuel had gotten caught up in what Saul looked like. The issue was one of: black, white, male and female. He was about to cast his vote for the wrong person. *It wasn't Samuel's vote, it was God's vote* that Samuel had, but because of his familiarity, he failed to see as God sees.

God immediately corrected Samuel and said to him, "Do not look on his countenance or his height of stature (outside) because I have refused him. I don't see as man sees because man looks on the outside but I look on the heart (inside)." This process continued as seven of Jesse's sons appeared before Samuel. Still, the Lord did not choose (vote) for any of these. On the outside, many of them had the physical qualifications, but on the inside none of them did.

Samuel must have been in a state of confusion, knowing that God had sent him to Jesse's house to anoint the next king of Israel among his sons. Perplexed, he asked Jesse if all of his sons were present. Jesse, as if he had forgotten about the other one, says, "I have one more, but it can't be him. He is out keeping the sheep and I'm sure he smells like them too." Samuel insists that they go and get him and declared that they would not sit down until they did so.

When David arrived, the Bible says that he was ruddy and of a beautiful countenance. The reference to his physical stature is again of significance because he did not look like Jesse's other sons, or like a person that God would anoint because he was black or white to be the next king of Israel. God can anoint a black man as well as he can anoint a white man and even a woman. The anointing belongs to God and He has the right to anoint any human that He chooses to because all men are created in His image and after His likeness.

The Bible says that when David came, the Lord said unto Samuel, "This is the Lord's anointed," and he arose and poured the oil on the head of David and the spirit of God came on David from that day forward. Samuel had to see past the physical and look into the spiritual; which is the mind of God to see what God was seeing. God always looks at the heart of his creation.

A man after God's own heart is a man who has a heart that God can turn. King Solomon said that the king's heart is in the Lord's hand and He (God) turns it wherever He wants to (Proverbs 21:1). It is crucial that you as a Christian be a person after God's own heart and be obedient to what He tells you and vote for the person who has a heart God can turn. This is called voting following your conscience; voting based on your own personal encounter with God just as Samuel did. Seek to find God's heart and vote following His heart. This is how your conscience (the ability to know what's right and what's wrong) was established. It was established in righteousness, from the mind of God. If my heart condemns me, God is greater than my heart. The voice of God will never make you violate His word or your conscience.

How Would Jesus Vote?

CHAPTER 12
YOU MUST HAVE A
REVELATION

The Lord Jesus had a similar situation when choosing his disciples as we have in choosing the next elected officials. The Bible says that He went up into a mountain to pray and He continued there all night. (Luke 6:12-13) There are several references where Jesus went into a mountain alone to pray to seek God's mind, once taking Peter, James and John with Him. (Luke 9:28) It was during these times that the Father God would give Jesus insight into what He was purposed to do.

These were the times that He was given some very important revelations. Revelation is defined as *the disclosure of truth or instruction concerning things before unknown.*

In Luke 6:7-16, after the Lord had just finished healing a man who had a withered hand, He went up into a mountain to pray. While there, similar to Moses, He got caught up in communion and fellowship with the Father and stayed there all night long. After communing with the Father all night long, the Bible says that when He came down from the mountain, He chose the twelve men that would be called His disciples. These twelve were chosen from among several (disciples). What made these twelve so special for the Lord to choose (vote) them. The previous lifestyles of many of these men would cause some concern on the part of the person who had to make the choice (vote).

The Lord Jesus was able to choose the twelve from among the many disciples because He spent quality time in fellowship and communion with the Father. Because of this, He had the *disclosure of truth and instructions concerning things before unknown.* He was given a *revelation.* As previously stated, Jesus did not depend on what had been the previous lifestyles of those men. Nothing that they had done in the past or what they were doing at that moment mattered. What was important is where they were going according to their God-given purpose, *therefore the revelation received by Jesus from His Father disallowed the past lifestyles of those men to be a current issue that would cause confusion and prevent him from following the* **counsel that He received from the Father.**

Who would choose (vote for) a man like Peter, who admitted that he was a sinful man, a man who eventually lied and denied that he knew Jesus? Who would choose a man like Matthew, who was an employee of the Roman government as a tax collector. The tax-collectors were permitted by the government to demand from the tax payers more than they were responsible to pay. Matthew was a thief among his own people. And finally, who would choose a Judas Iscariot, a man who had difficulty being loyal to his covenant relationships. He stole money from Jesus and sold Jesus for 30 pieces of silver to the Jewish leadership and they in turn crucified Him. God only knows the storied past of the other nine disciples. Despite all of this the Lord Jesus chose (voted for) all twelve. How did He do it and why did He do it? The answer is obvious. He had a revelation.

How would Jesus Vote?

Another case involving the Lord Jesus in choosing a leader was him choosing Saul of Tarsus who later became Paul the Apostle-one of the most dynamic of all the disciples. A background check would have turned up that he was a high ranking official among the Pharisees.

The Pharisees were an elite group among the religious sects in Israel. After the Lord had ascended up into heaven, His influence began to spread throughout the known world. A new culture was being established all over the world with Jesus as the focal point. (If I be lifted up I'll draw all men to me) Peter and some of the others had been threatened by these same Pharisees not to teach or to preach in the name of Jesus because it was through that name that great signs, wonders, and miracles were happening and the Pharisees witnessed that Jesus was indeed raised from the dead and that He was legislating righteousness through those who had learned of Him and received His yoke. Stephen was such a man. He gave great witness to the Lord Jesus and it cost him his life. He and others suffered for Christ's sake but they couldn't stop because it had become their conscience authority to follow the ways of Jesus and they were driven by the authority of their conscious, the Lord Jesus.

Saul was committed to follow his conscience authority as well, which said that anyone or anything that was opposing the religious order established by Moses had to be punished. These followers of this Jesus had to be stopped at any cost. Because of this, Saul requested permission to round up anyone who believed in Jesus and practiced what He taught. It did not matter the race, gender or the age, they all had to be stopped. In Acts 8:1-3, he was a satisfied witness at the stoning of Steven.

And Saul was consenting unto his death. And at that time there was a great persecution against the

church which was at Jerusalem; and they were all
scattered abroad throughout the regions of Judaea
and Samaria, except the apostles. As for SAUL,
he made havock of the church, entering into every
house, and haling men and women committed them
to prison.

In Acts 9:1, we read,
And Saul, yet breathing out threatening's and slaughter
against the disciples of the Lord, went unto the high
priest, and desired of him letters to Damascus to the
synagogues, that if he found any of this way, whether
they were men or women, he might bring them bound
unto Jerusalem.

With his written permission, he set out on his mission. However, the mission experienced a great interrupting; one that would change Saul's life forever.

The church must choose the next elected officials of our government, whether local, state or federal. Those to choose from in many of these places do not present a choice that would make the Father's heart glad. In other words, many of the candidates have chosen not to follow God's way of doing things. The unfortunate event of not having righteous candidates to make choosing much easier is a tragedy in and of itself. But we're still faced with the responsibility of voting. Saul was a man who was attempting to destroy that which God had established. He was on a mission and was succeeding in his efforts. Jesus interrupts him, not for Saul's sake but for the Lords sake.

There are many in the church today who are having their conscience fragmented. The media's efforts to present all the negative things that each of the candidates have done or is doing has can have a negative effect on all those who listen. Whether, Christian or non-Christian, black or white, etc... Jesus said in Mark 4:24 to be careful how you hear because *how you* hear will determine *what* you really hear, and what you really hear will eventually affect your decision-making ability. When you talk to the average Christian about any election they will usually rehearse what they've heard through the different media outlets which are usually according to their traditional way of interpreting the political process. And what they've heard is causing them to settle into a particular political position.

In the story of Saul, there is a great parallel truth that I believe will help the Christian understand that they must have a revelation. In Acts 9:8-20, we see that after Saul was interrupted by the Lord, he was given the instruction to proceed into Damascus.

And Saul arose from the earth; and when his eyes were opened, he saw no man: but they led him by the hand, and brought him into Damascus. And he was three days without sight, and neither did eat nor drink. And there was a certain disciple at Damascus, named Ananias; and to him said the Lord in a vision, Ananias. And he said, Behold, I am here, Lord. And the Lord said unto him, Arise, and go into the street which is called Straight, and inquire in the house of Judas for one called Saul, of Tarsus: for, behold, he prayeth, And hath seen in a vision a man named Ananias coming in, and putting his hand on him, that he might receive his sight. Then Ananias answered, Lord, I have heard by many of this man, how much evil he hath done to thy saints at Jerusalem: And here he hath authority from the chief priests to bind all that call on thy name. But the Lord said unto him, Go thy way: for he is a chosen vessel unto me, to bear my name before the Gentiles, and kings, and the children of Israel: For I will show him how great things he must suffer for my name's sake. And Ananias went his way, and entered into the house; and putting his hands on him said, Brother Saul, the Lord, even Jesus, that appeared unto thee in the way as thou camest, hath sent me; that thou mightest receive thy sight, and be filled with the Holy

Ghost. And immediately there fell from his eyes as it had been scales: and he received sight forthwith, and arose, and was baptized. And when he had received meat, he was strengthened. Then was Saul certain days with the disciples which were at Damascus. And straightway he preached Christ in the synagogues, that he is the Son of God.

There was a disciple named Ananias whom the Lord would use to validate his choice to use Saul for his service. But Ananias response was one of which had been developed by what he had heard from the Jerusalem media about this Saul of Tarsus. God is talking but Ananias cannot hear what He is saying because he had been listening to the wrong voices. (polarized, brainwashed) Ananias's perception had been marred because of what he had heard. What he had heard had become his conscience authority and this made him content to disobey a command from his Lord. In Acts 9:13-16, we read:

Then Ananias answered, Lord, ***I have heard by many of this man****, how much evil he hath done to thy saints at Jerusalem: And here he hath authority from the chief priests to bind all that call on thy name, But the Lord said unto him, Go thy way: for he is a chosen vessel unto me, to bear my name before the Gentiles, and kings, and the children of Israel: For I will show him how great things he must suffer for my name's sake.*

It wasn't Ananias's choice to choose Saul. Saul wasn't Ananias's chosen vessel, he was the Lord's chosen vessel. Saul was the Lord's choice. Ananias finally received the revelation he needed to obey the Lord and he eventually did. We continue to read in Acts 9:17-18

And Ananias went his way, and entered into the house; and putting his hands on him said, Brother Saul, the Lord, even Jesus, that appeared unto thee in the way as thou camest, hath sent me, that thou mightest receive thy sight, and be filled with the Holy Ghost. And immediately there fell from his eyes as it had been scales:

Saul went from being an outrageous persecutor of the gospel of Christ to be an illustrious professor and preacher of it, filled with the Holy Ghost and a man of great revelation. The New Testament bears the evidence of Ananias's obedience to the revelation he received from the Lord concerning Saul. He later became Paul the Apostle and great revelator. He proved what he preached and became one of the most prolific authors among the New Testament writers. God knew the heart of Saul of Tarsus, even though he was trying to destroy the plan of God. God saw in him that which was necessary to promote and do the will of God.

In these trying times, the church must gain the revelation needed to accurately vote as God would have us to. We must position ourselves to infiltrate each sphere of influence in this nation much like the world has infiltrated the church. Like the world, we must pursue getting involved in the political process with violent aggression according to God's standards and not the world's. We must find ourselves in the positions throughout the nation to either vote for someone who will legislate righteousness or become the person who others of like faith hearing the same voice will vote for. Only then will the church be what it is in reality, light and salt.

This is How Jesus Would Vote!

Conclusion

In 2 Chronicles 21, Jehoshaphat was faced with a dilemma that would mean the destruction of his people and the nation of Israel. He set out to get some instructions from God by calling a solemn fast for himself and the people. His desire to know the will of God concerning his situation caused God to show up on his behalf and give him the victory.

I would encourage you to set yourself to seek God's face concerning upcoming elections. Even as Jehoshaphat had a victorious outcome, I too believe that America can remain a blessed nation. Please pray this with me.

Heavenly Father I bless you and give you all the praise due your Holy name. I ask you to forgive me for abdicating my responsibilities as it relates to the political process and failing to seek your face in the matter of voting. I ask you to give me the courage to seek your face so that I might find your heart. I understand how crucial this election is and also my role as your instrument. My role has to be fulfilled on my part. I choose to hear your voice in this matter and I refuse to follow any other voice. I will not vote for the black man just because he's black and a democrat neither will I vote for the white man just because he's white and a Republican? I will vote for the person to whom you tell me to vote for. This will be the person whose heart you will be able to turn for your own purposes. I thank you for allowing me the opportunity of partnering with you in this process. In Jesus' name I pray, Amen